Picture Perfect Frame

By Lynn Cahoon

The Tourist Trap Mysteries
Picture Perfect Frame
Murder in Waiting
Memories and Murder
Killer Party
Hospitality and Homicide
Tea Cups and Carnage
Murder on Wheels
Killer Run
Dressed to Kill
If the Shoe Kills
Mission to Murder
Guidebook to Murder

Novellas
A Very Mummy Holiday
Mother's Day Mayhem
Corned Beef and Casualties
Santa Puppy
A Deadly Brew
Rockets' Dead Glare

The Kitchen Witch Mysteries
One Poison Pie

Novellas
Chili Cauldron Curse

The Farm-to-Fork Mysteries
One Potato, Two Potato, Dead
Killer Green Tomatoes
Who Moved My Goat Cheese?

Deep Fried Revenge

Picture Perfect Frame

Lynn Cahoon

LYRICAL UNDERGROUND
Kensington Publishing Corp.
www.kensingtonbooks.com

LYRICAL UNDERGROUND BOOKS are published by
Kensington Publishing Corp.
119 West 40th Street
New York, NY 10018

All Kensington titles, imprints, and distributed lines are available at special quantity discounts for bulk purchases for sales promotion, premiums, fund-raising, educational, or institutional use.

Special book excerpts or customized printings can also be created to fit specific needs. For details, write or phone the office of the Kensington Sales Manager: Kensington Publishing Corp., 119 West 40th Street, New York, NY 10018. Attn. Sales Department. Phone: 1-800-221-2647.

Lyrical Underground and Lyrical Underground logo Reg. US Pat. & TM Off.

First Electronic Edition: March 2021
ISBN-13: 978-1-5161-0306-5 (ebook)
ISBN-10: 1-5161-0306-8 (ebook)

First Print Edition: March 2021
ISBN-13: 978-1-5161-0309-6
ISBN-10: 1-5161-0309-2

Printed in the United States of America

To Kathy—you were the first friend I could tell my wild dreams and you believed they could come true. You believed in me. Thank you.

ACKNOWLEDGMENTS

This book was written during the virus crisis of 2020. I don't know what the world will look like when it's published—March 2021—but I'm hoping you won't judge me through my writing the world that was. A world where South Cove still puts on St. Patrick's Day street festivals and gatherings of more than ten are not only welcome, but encouraged. I hope in 2021 we are kinder to each other—knowing that as it's ever been—life is fragile and should be lived with joy and exuberance.

Big thanks to my publisher, who made work from home work. My editor, who gave me grace and support during this time. And my agent, who kept pushing me to do me.

Chapter 1

"Creation is the heart of art. No matter if the product isn't quite what you want, the act of creation is one of rejuvenation. People need to celebrate not only the successes of their work, but their failures as well." Meredith Cole glanced around the Coffee, Books, and More shop, crowded with Business-to-Business attendees. Her sharp features made her straight red hair stand out even more. And her green eyes were narrowed and focused on the audience. No one would ever call this woman warm and fuzzy. But somehow, her message and her voice felt soft and encouraging as she continued. "No matter what our job entails, we are all artists and creators inside."

Spring had finally arrived in the coastal California town, or at least spring without rain. The sun was shining, the birds singing, and after our newest business owner finished with her talk on *Why Art Matters*, the group of small business owners would be brainstorming marketing events for the upcoming months. A topic I was much more invested in than getting in touch with my creative side.

"Maybe you have one deep, deep inside you." Toby Killian leaned across the table and refilled my coffee mug. His strong jaw and dark, short hair made him look more like one of the romance novel cover models than a coffee shop barista. Of course, his other job was as a South Cove police officer, so he did have that hero attitude. "Didn't Jackie take decorating the store off your list of chores after the last Valentine's disaster?"

"Purple and black are totally appropriate Valentine's colors in my mind." I grinned at my part-time barista. Toby had been my first employee not related to me. Aunt Jackie had been the first, and even though I'd thought it had been a temporary offer of help so many years ago, my aunt was still here. Well, she would be here as soon as she and Harrold got back from their long weekend in Arizona. "Did Jackie call off for tonight yet?"

Toby shook his head. "I haven't heard from her. Do you need me to stay?"

"Shh." A woman across the table leaned over and gave us both a look of disgust. "I'm trying to listen."

"We'll talk later." Toby gave the shusher one of his winning smiles and left me alone.

Amy Newman, my best friend and South Cove's receptionist, city planner, and meeting notetaker, giggled. Amy looked like she belonged in the central coastal community. Her short, blond hair sparkled against her always tanned face. If she'd been in a bikini and holding her board, she'd make a perfect beach promotional shot. Yes, my best friend was a surfer. But I didn't hold that against her. Much.

The woman who had shushed us was one of the artists who had opened a studio last year on Main Street. I had no idea what her name was because this was the first meeting she'd attended. Art supports art, I guessed. I started making notes about what I needed to get done today just in case I needed to step in for the evening shift.

After a very hearty round of applause when Meredith finished, Darla Taylor took the podium. If Amy was the image of an athletic life, Darla was the "before" picture. Even after making a habit of working out with her boyfriend, Darla still was more fluff than muscle. She was friendly and welcoming, an attitude that served her well as the owner/manager of South Cove Winery. We were friends and I gave her a big smile to let her know I was listening. Well, at least to her.

"Good morning, South Cove. I'm so glad you're here today. We're finishing up the final touches on our St. Patrick's Day event. No parade this year, but we'll have Main Street blocked off for a street fair so we can bring our businesses out on Main Street. Literally." She grinned as she continued. "What we need to talk about today is Easter. I know we've gone back and forth on this, but I'd still like to have a B2B-sponsored egg hunt the Saturday before. If you're out of town, that's fine, but remember this the next time we come asking for something."

"Darla, where can we sign up to help with the egg hunt?" Amy raised her hand, asking the question before Darla could respond. "I love working with kids."

"Of course you do," I grumbled at my friend.

Amy grabbed my arm and lifted it in the air. "Jill volunteers to help as well."

Darla took out three clipboards and passed them to the person sitting to her right. "Sounds perfect. I'm passing out sign-up sheets for the next three events. I've added a May Flowers Festival as well as a June wedding event where we're bringing in some highly qualified wedding planners, florists, and caterers for your enjoyment. This event will be at the community center, and all the bed-and-breakfast owners are giving away a free weekend stay to bring in visitors."

"That sounds wonderful." Amy literally purred. "I know I'll be spending all day at the event."

I stared at my friend. "You already have your entire wedding planned. And the ceremony will be over by then anyway. You're getting married the end of the month."

"Don't say that, you'll jinx it." Amy didn't meet my gaze. "Plans change. Look at your aunt and Harrold. They were going to do a big wedding in the city and instead visited an Elvis impersonator. Besides, I don't think Justin has picked out a honeymoon destination yet. If he's not committed to something by then, I'm dragging him in that gym with me and making him sign up for something with the travel agent from Bakerstown."

"Not the most cooperative way to start a marriage, but you do you." I understood where my friend was coming from and I was pretty sure she wouldn't actually do it. Or at least I hoped. It has been a long engagement.

Darla glanced around the room, watching to see who was signing up on what clipboard. "If there aren't any questions, I'll send out emails to the new committees and I'll see all of you at the St. Patrick's Day Street Fair."

"Sounds fun." The artist who'd shushed me gave Darla a big grin and started to stand.

"Jill, did you want to close the meeting?" Darla glanced at me because I ran the meetings for the City Council, but I waved her off. It was time to get back to my real job, running Coffee, Books, and More, the only coffee shop–bookstore in the area. Darla picked up the wooden gavel we used to start and end the meetings and cracked it on the podium. "Then we're adjourned."

As we moved table and chairs to get my dining room back in order, Evie Marshall, our newest barista and my new renter for the apartment above the shop came in the front door. Her green eyes scanned the room as she walked around the scattered tables. She carried Homer, her tan Pom. He and Emma, my golden retriever, had met a few weekends ago at a barbecue at my house. They'd become fast friends.

"Sorry to bring him in this way, Jill." Evie stopped by where I'd been arranging a table. "I forgot to grab my keys when I went out and the back door locked on me."

Homer reached his neck so he could sniff me. I swear, the dog could smell a cookie crumb or treat from a mile away. I rubbed between his ears and focused on Evie. She had her hair in tiny braids, each one with at least one colored bead weaved in. She looked great in sweats and no makeup. I should have hated her for that alone, but she was an amazing barista and had a wide knowledge of books too. And she was nice. "No worries. Evie, have you met our newest business owner here in South Cove? This is Meredith Cole."

"So nice to meet you." Meredith reached out to pet Homer, but a small growl emitted from the dog's throat. "Sorry, I should have asked first."

"He's usually great with strangers. Maybe he's just had too much change lately." Evie pulled him closer to her chest and put her hand over his nose to keep him from actually biting the newcomer.

"Totally my bad. I was raised with dogs. I should know better." Meredith flashed Evie a smile, then turned to me. "I was just making sure you were coming tonight. Neal and I are buying the wine this afternoon, so I wanted to get a solid head count. You and your guy, Greg, right?"

I nodded. As long as there wasn't a crazy problem that kept him at the station, we'd be there. "I'm coming. And Greg's onboard. Unless something happens."

"Remind me. He's a firefighter?"

Amy snorted. "Nope. Greg's our local police detective. He should be police chief, but Mayor Baylor keeps shooting down the title change. He's afraid Greg's going to challenge him for his mayoral spot."

"Oh, that's right." Meredith turned to Amy. "You and your fiancé are coming, right?"

"Our first date night for a while. Justin's been crazy busy with midterms over at the university for the last few weeks." Amy put the last chair under the table by where we were standing. "You and Neal are married, right? Did you get married locally? What was your venue?"

I giggled and Amy threw me a dirty look. "Sorry, but I'm glad you have a new victim in this whole marriage insanity."

Darla picked up all three clipboards and tucked them into her tote. "I was going to mention that Matt's not going to be able to come. He's in Missouri at his folks' house doing some sort of farm stuff. Plowing or planting or something. He's told me, but I keep forgetting. I don't even have a garden or an inside plant. He really shouldn't expect me to follow his discussion on crop raising."

"Darla, a farm wife." I tried out the image. It didn't take. Although the girl was so crazy in love with her boyfriend, Matt, I wouldn't put it past her to at least try.

"Don't start. Anyway, sorry about the late notice." She turned away from me and focused on Meredith.

"No problem." Meredith glanced at Evie. "Do you want to come? We're set up for ten—the guy who runs the antique shop is bringing his girlfriend and a couple who's staying at Main Street Bed and Breakfast this week."

Evie's eyes widened. "Me? You're inviting me to the party?"

"Free of charge. I need to get some karma going around here and I'd rather not bring in just anyone." She looked around the room. "Some of the local artists are kind of touchy when you talk about teaching others how to paint. Everyone has an opinion. Like they're all Degas or Monet. I've visited most of the galleries here, and although they do a great job in seascapes, I'm certain no one is going to break out and take over the art world."

I decided right there and then that I liked Meredith. I had always thought our artist members of the business to business group were a bit too in love with themselves. Meredith seemed down-to-earth and a great judge of character. "Evie, you need to come. It will be a great way to meet other people in South Cove."

"I like the people I know. I'd hate to risk fate." Evie glanced around the shop, now put back together for the day's business. Her grip tightened on Homer, who'd stopped growling but was still watching Meredith closely. "I'll think about it. What time?"

"It starts about six thirty. Greg doesn't like to be out late on a work night." I glanced over at Toby, who was behind the counter. A line was starting to form. Most of the students from the cosmetology school were here for their morning break. "I need to go help Toby. See you all tonight. Evie, I'll stop at the apartment if you want to walk over with us."

"I do need to get out. So, yes, that would be perfect. Thank you." Evie moved toward the back door to the apartment. "I might have to take a break to check on Homer. He's having some problems adjusting."

"Oh no." I rubbed the little dog's chin. "Are you homesick, Homer?"

"No, he's not. Neither one of us are." Evie turned on her heel and stomped toward the back door.

I watched her leave before asking the group, "Did I say something wrong?"

"Not that I heard. Maybe she's just a little nervous about leaving the dog?" Amy put her hand on my shoulder. "Don't worry about it. We're just getting to know one another. You know that process takes some time. She moved from a house on an acre outside of New York City; living here in an apartment must be a total change."

I glanced at the line, which seemed to be even longer, so I excused myself and went to help Toby. But my thoughts were stuck on Evie. Was she going to fit in? Was this just an isolated incident or would our customer service suffer from her verbal snaps?

Amy turned down meeting for lunch when she came to say goodbye. She was driving into the city to meet Justin that afternoon because Mayor Baylor and his wife, Tina, were off on a cruise. From what I saw, our mayor did a lot of vacationing under the guise of networking and promotion. I wasn't sure people who cruised were actually small-town coastal tourists. But he somehow convinced the Council.

After the rush had left I picked up an Advanced Reader Copy one of the book publicists in New York had sent us. I loved this mystery author and decided to snatch the book before my aunt even realized it had arrived. I was about to call her when Deek Kerr came in the front door, his laptop case over his shoulder. Today his blond cornrows were dyed green. He set down his stuff at a table near the wall where he could plug in his computer and then strolled behind the bar. "What are you doing here?"

He filled a large mug with coffee and then sprinkled some cinnamon on top. He glanced at the clock before answering me. "For the next three hours I am writing and hope to get this chapter done. I so hate the middle. I know everyone told me it would be the pits, but did I listen? No. I did not."

I glanced at the schedule we had sitting by the cash register. Deek wasn't working until tomorrow, when he took over for me, unless he'd taken Aunt Jackie's shift. "After you pen your opus, what then?"

"Then I try to fill your aunt's shoes. Do you know she listed off all the things I needed to do on 'her shift' and made me repeat them after her? When she tried a second time I politely reminded her that she was asking me for a favor. She shut up after that. Although I think her new hubby hung up the phone, not her. She was ready to give me the what's for." Deek grinned as he walked back to his table. "I like your new uncle. He's got moxie."

"Okay then." I wished my aunt had called me to deal with this but, typical Jackie, she had to handle everything on her own. Even setting up coverage for her shift when her vacation went long.

"She doesn't like to bother you. It makes her feel weak," Deek said without looking up from his laptop.

"Stop reading my thoughts. I may have some X-rated things up there I don't want you to know." I filled a travel mug with ice and poured tea over the top. Then I chose a cookie for the walk home. I could stop at Diamond Lille's for lunch, but without Amy to chat with, I'd rather go home and cuddle with Emma.

"I don't read minds, I read auras. Besides, you're too much of an open book. Even if I tried, I wouldn't be able to stop. You throw up these billboard-size messages." He glanced up from the screen. "Besides, if the two of you would just talk, I wouldn't have to act like Apollo and transport messages."

I paused by his spot on the way out the door. I'd already said goodbye to Toby. He was stocking the dessert case. The group from the meeting had cleaned out the treats to take home for afternoon snacks. Which was another reason I let the group meet at my place. It increased sales once a month. The worse the news from the City Council on fees and zoning issues, the better my sales went that day.

"Well, I'm just glad you're here to translate. With you, Greg, and Harrold as buffers, I may never have to talk to her again." I glanced at the screen. "Page 205? I thought you were on page 250 yesterday?"

"I threw away a scene. My professor didn't like where it was going." Deek slumped in his seat. "I can't believe books get written when there's so many opinions involved in every step."

"Want a piece of advice I heard along the way?"

He nodded. "Sure. Your advice is usually just what I need to hear. I'm thinking you're the author whisperer."

"Heaven help me. That would be awful." I shook the idea off me like it was a sticky cobweb. "Anyway, what I heard was you never let anyone read the first draft until you're done."

"That won't work. Professor Hogan makes us turn in pages every week." Deek leaned back his head. "Paper copies that he gives back with red ink all over them."

"That doesn't seem helpful." I thought about the lectures I'd heard from a lot of authors doing tour talks. "Okay, this one is better. Don't throw away anything. Keep it separate. You realize that once you get your grade on the class, you're going to have to be the one to take a risk and find an agent. Your professor won't be there to judge your work. You should keep what speaks to you."

He stared at me. "You're telling me to keep two sets of books? One just for the professor and one that would be the real book?"

"That way you won't hurt the guy's feelings, and by the time it gets published, time will have passed and you can blame the publisher's editors for the changes."

"That's genius. I can pretend I agree, but not really."

I nodded. "That could be true."

"You're doing it right now, aren't you?" Deek grinned as he returned to his keyboard. "Is that what you do to your aunt?"

"I don't know what you mean." I waved at Toby and left the shop, heading home to an afternoon cuddled with Emma and the new book. Life was good.

"Miss Gardner? I need to talk to you about the way the business meetings are being run. Darla Taylor is always pushing her own agenda, and it always benefits her winery more than other businesses in town. Exactly what am I going to drag out on the street to sell to drunk green people?" Josh Thomas stared at me as I paused by his antiques shop where he stood, sweeping the already clean sidewalk. "Maybe a priceless set of Queen Anne dishware or some crystal? I'll lose more in people dropping things than I'll sell."

And as it does sometimes, life turned from good to crap with one conversation.

Chapter 2

By the time I got home, I was starving. I'd spent at least an hour assuring Josh that the marketing planning wasn't just set up to benefit Darla's winery and spent time brainstorming ideas on what his store could sell during the event. Kyle Nabors, Josh's assistant, had jumped in at the end and taken over the planning for the upcoming event. Kyle had talked Josh into a leprechaun theme. I hoped he could pull this off, because if he didn't, I'd agreed to bring up Josh's concern with Darla and the Council. I didn't want to risk losing Darla as the spearhead of these festivals. She was a marketing genius. Josh just needed to be more open-minded and creative.

And I've heard you can teach pigs to fly.

I eyed the cookies on the counter, but instead took out meat, cheese, and other items to make myself a sandwich. I'd been eating way too many cookies and desserts from the store this winter and my pants were beginning to feel a little tight. I should run today too. I glanced at Emma, who was watching me make my lunch, and sighed.

Today was one of those days when what I wanted to do was coming up against what I needed to do. I had to be in the shower at five to be ready for the painting event at Drunken Art Studio because I had told Evie we'd meet her at six. If we ran, I'd only have two hours to read. If no one else stole some of my time.

Emma glanced at the doorway where her leash was hanging on a hook and back to me. She'd learned not even to look at the leash if it was raining. But she'd been outside since I'd come home and she knew it was a perfect day. Well, she would if she thought like me. I'm inclined to give my dog and other animals a little grace on what they were thinking. Which means I believe they think like we do. I ruffled her fur as I took the plate to the table. "Let me eat and then I'll fold that last load of clothes I didn't get done yesterday. Then we'll run."

Emma let out a short yip, then went to lay down on her kitchen bed to wait. And who says dogs can't understand you?

I glanced at the mail while I ate, sorting it into two piles: bills and junk. And one invitation. The bright blue of the envelope made me smile as I opened it. Olivia was turning six and having a princess party at one of the city's popular kid pizza spots. Olivia was Sasha's daughter, a former employee of Coffee, Books, and More, and a friend. A note had been added to the envelope and I opened the letter to read it.

Dear Jill, I hope this finds you and all my friends in South Cove well. Thank you for hiring Evie. She's a great person and will fit right in, or will as soon as she deals with some demons from the past. I believe South Cove is an excellent place for people to find their true calling. Like I did. Hope to see you at the party. If Toby wants to come and bring a date, Olivia would love to see him. Sasha.

Toby. My barista and part-time deputy had carried a torch for Sasha and Olivia for a long time after they left South Cove to start a new life. He still hadn't started dating anyone seriously since the breakup. I wasn't sure attending Olivia's party and seeing their new life with a new man was in his best interest. But I'd talk to Greg to see if I should pass on Sasha's note. She could have just sent Toby an invitation. She knew how to reach him. I hated being in the middle of this.

Relationships were hard. Relationships and past relationships in a small town were impossible to just step away from. There was always someone who liked to bring up your past and your past mistakes. I tucked away the invitation in my planner and put a note in the calendar on the day of the party. I'd at least send Olivia a book basket from the store. Pushing the reading button was not only good for society but also my livelihood. Besides, I knew Sasha kept the girl busy with books. It was something in our blood.

I went upstairs, changed, and brought down a load of laundry to start. It was time to run and forget about everything except the taste of the salt air on my lips and the feel of the cool breeze that would cool me down as I ran. Emma had her own running joys, like playing in the surf and chasing away the seagulls from the shoreline. I had to face the fact that we were both addicted to our shoreline lifestyle. I hoped I never had to leave.

I'd had a bit of a scare a few months before, when a developer wanted, badly, to buy my house. But I'd dealt with that. My fear was that he wouldn't be the last to come with suitcases filled with money to purchase my house or the property around it. I had to face the fact that the area was starting to grow. And things around me would change. I just had to keep a level head on me and not worry about a random future.

Traffic into town and on Highway 1 was light as we crossed to the beach parking lot. Early spring meant we didn't get a lot of weekday visitors to town, which was great for me. I loved it being a little quiet, even though my aunt bemoaned our financial future every off-season. This year she'd been too busy setting up her new life to badger me. Something I blessed Harrold for every morning. We hit the sand, and because there wasn't anyone in sight, I unclipped Emma's leash. She'd stay nearby and come back when I called. And she knew to stay away from sea lions after having a bit of a scare when she was a pup. Now, she'd let me know one was nearby with a short bark and then she'd run next to me. Like I could save her from the massive beast.

I love that my dog thinks I'm a superhero.

We were on the way back when I saw someone walking toward us. I was about to clip on Emma's leash when she took off running toward the figure. It had to be someone we knew or she would have stayed next to me. I kept up my pace and, as I grew closer, realized it was Greg walking toward us.

"Hey, handsome, what are you doing off work?" I stopped running as I reached him and leaned in for a kiss.

He obliged, then took Emma's leash from me and clipped it on her collar. "Just keeping the beach safe from random loose dogs and running women."

"Did someone call with a complaint?" I glanced around the beach, which was still empty except for us and the sandpipers playing in the waves.

"No. I'm just giving you my standard beach protocol speech. On your way home? Can I walk with you?" He fell in step with me and I got a bad feeling.

"Okay, so what happened?"

He jerked his head toward me and frowned. "What do you mean?"

"You never come walk me home from a run. Either there's a serial-killing clown in the area or you had a run-in at work. Probably with the mayor. Nope, he's on a cruise." I took his hand in mine as we walked. "Tell Jill all about your troubles and maybe I can fix them."

"I don't know if you can fix this one. Esmeralda's talking about quitting." He glanced up at the bluff, where my house stood. Esmeralda lived across the street, just up from the farmers market stand that had been built a few years before. During the off-season the stand was only open on the weekends, so today it stood boarded up and silent.

"Why? Don't tell me she's moving?" I liked my neighbor. Well, once I got past the freak-out I had when she did her woo-woo fortune-telling stuff on me. I didn't mind the fact that she made her living telling people messages from beyond. Well, that and being a part-time dispatcher for Greg at the police station.

"I don't think so. She said something about it not being fair that she was taking a job from one of the other townspeople who needed it. It was a strange conversation. I'm not sure exactly what she wants." He sighed as we climbed the stairs. "I know I can get along without her. We'll hire someone and train them. But I like working with her. She has a good head on her shoulders and isn't afraid of telling me when I'm off on a wrong track."

I considered Greg's dilemma. I knew I hated losing people from the shop, but they usually quit to go on to better things. Like Sasha. And Nick, my friend Sadie's kid, who stopped working summers for us because he started doing financial internships at college. He'd spent last summer working in London. This summer he was probably getting his first adult job and moving away to his new life. Those kinds of losses were easy for me to deal with because it was for a better life. This felt off. Like Esmeralda was listening to the wrong voice and not taking her own needs into consideration. "I could talk to her if you want me to."

Greg's face lit up and I realized that was why he'd come to find me. He wanted me to fix this. "That would be great."

I groaned inwardly. I did want to help my boyfriend with his employee troubles, but honestly, it wasn't my business. He should be the one to convince Esmeralda to stay, not me. "I really don't think she needs my input on this. You should be the one to talk to her."

"I will. I promise. But if you could just lay the groundwork for me? I'd appreciate it." He paused as we looked both ways, then looked again. Then he changed the subject. "I proposed a walk light to the City Council again this year. I'm hoping it makes it to the budget. The state has safety grants that will pay most of the cost. Marvin's shot it down three years in a row to put more money into his mayoral budget. This year, I feel lucky."

As we climbed the hill to my—I meant, our house, because Greg lived with me—I glanced over at Esmeralda's place. She was home and a black BMW convertible was parked in the driveway. Esmeralda always kept her Land Rover parked in the garage. I think she didn't want her clients to know what her financial situation was; maybe it made for larger tips if they thought she was struggling. I knew she'd bought the SUV new and for cash because she'd given me the name of the dealership in Bakerstown when I bought my new Jeep a few years ago. He'd given her a discount for an all-cash offer.

But nothing else about the woman screamed money. Her house was a replica of mine, having been built the same year by the same builder. And although housing prices were crazy high where we lived, you didn't get that money unless you decided to sell. Something neither of us were willing to do.

As we walked inside our house, I realized this was the second time that day I'd been put into a position I didn't want to be in. A discussion that wasn't mine to have had been placed at my door and I'd volunteered to take on at least the one. As we got settled in the kitchen, I took out Sasha's invite and tossed it to him on the table. "Do you want to go?"

"Hmmm, spend an afternoon locked in a room with screaming kids and loud noises?" He glanced at the invite again. "I'll have to check my work calendar."

"It's on a Saturday and there will be pizza." I took two sodas out of the fridge. "And maybe video games."

"I can have pizza, video games, and beer if I stay home. I feel like this is something that people with kids do. I'll go if you want to be there, but really, driving a couple of hours to be somewhere for an hour isn't really a great way to spend my day off." He glanced at the date and put his hands on his face like that kid in the old movie. "Oh no, I can't go. That's the street fair weekend. I can't take off and leave my crew on their own to round up drunken leprechauns."

"You're a good boss. Have you thought about hiring on another person?" I set the soda on the table and slipped onto a chair. "I think you'd already decided not to go when I brought it up."

"I'd like to get Toby on full-time first. Then Tim needs a full-time gig. Tim and his girl are getting married next June. Toby told me to move Tim up on the list because of the wedding, but that's not fair. Toby has seniority and he'll be the first one to go full-time. As soon as the mayor approves more staff hours." He ignored my comment about Sasha's party. He ran a hand through his hair. "I hate dealing with the administrative part of this. One more reason I don't want to lose Esmeralda. I'm pretty sure she takes care of things I don't even realize need fixing."

"Stop, I already said I'd talk to her." I closed my eyes. "Aunt Jackie called off for her shift today. Of course she didn't call me. She just made other arrangements."

"She probably didn't want to worry you. And she knew you'd cover the shift rather than ask one of the others to do it." He handed the invitation back to me. "My vote is no, but I'll go if you want to see Sasha."

"I would love to see Sasha and Olivia, but not in a mess of other kids I don't know. Besides, since you brought up the street festival, I've realized I can't take off that weekend either. Maybe we could go up sometime next month and spend the weekend in town. We take Olivia to the zoo or something fun, then have dinner and really talk." I was beginning to brighten up. This was a good, no, a great plan.

He stood and kissed me on the forehead. "I'm running upstairs to change, then I'll meet you at the thing tonight. I've got some paperwork to finish at the station."

"What about dinner?"

He shrugged. "I'll call in for some chicken from Diamond Lille's. Do you want me to have them send you an order too?"

I glanced at the fridge, which I knew had plenty of food. Including tortellini soup I'd made last weekend. I had planned to serve it for dinner tonight; then I'd put the leftovers in the freezer for easy lunches. This just meant there would be more leftovers. "No, I'll have soup and salad for dinner. You can grill tomorrow night to make it up to me."

He laughed. "I'm not sure what I need to make amends for, but that's a plan."

I watched him head up the stairs, then found the book in my tote and my soda and headed for the couch. This gave me plenty of reading time. Right after I moved the clothes to the dryer, I reminded myself.

I'd gotten lost in the book, but Emma nudged my foot at about four, reminding me about dinner. Okay, so maybe she was telling me she had to go outside, but it served the same purpose. I put a serving of the soup on to heat and packed the rest into freezer containers. Then I made a quick salad while the soup was on the stove. Ten minutes later Emma was back in the house and I was sitting down for dinner.

A knock came on the door and I moved the food back over to the counter where Emma couldn't reach it. When I opened the door Esmeralda stood there. "Hey, come in."

She shook her head and the bells on her head scarf jingled. "Look, I just came over to tell you …"

I watched as she stared at me. I knew that look. Something else was going on. "What? What's wrong? Are you having a vision?"

"You don't believe in visions." She put a hand on the doorframe and took a deep breath, obviously in distress.

"Seriously, you don't look good. Come inside and sit down. I'm worried about you. Should I call the ambulance?" I reached out and touched her arm, and a swirl of emotions hit me like a ton of bricks. My fingers jerked back. "What the heck was that?"

"Sorry, I'm in touch with the other side. I didn't do my cleansing ritual because I have another client in a few minutes." She straightened, and color came back into her face. "I just want you to know that I'm doing this for his own good. Just know that."

"Leaving the station? I'm supposed to talk you out of it." I watched her. She wanted to leave and sprint across the street. Emma whined behind me.

"I'm not sure you can do that." She turned and headed off the porch. "My client is almost here. I'll come by tomorrow to explain. I owe him that much, but I can't tell him why."

I was about to say no one was at her house when I saw a pair of headlights turn off Highway 1 and onto the street that ran into South Cove. Esmeralda beat the car there by seconds and stood in the doorway to greet the newcomers like she'd been home all along.

I closed the door and turned to Emma. "Our neighbor is going batty."

Emma stared at the door and whined again.

"I know, you felt it too." I walked back to the kitchen. Something bad was going on with Esmeralda and I was going to find out what. She might not be the perfect neighbor, but she was part of my South Cove family. No one was going to run her off her job.

I ate my dinner as I tried to get back into the story. But I couldn't stop thinking about Esmeralda and our conversation. Finally, I closed the book, cleaned up my dinner dishes, and went upstairs to get in the shower. Hopefully I'd be able to wash this funk off me so I'd be fun, creative Jill tonight.

Or at least fun Jill. Toby was right. I didn't have a creative bone in my body.

Chapter 3

Evie was sitting outside the coffee shop, reading, when I arrived. She'd dressed in a floral, flowing shirt and skinny jeans with wedge heels. I was in my favorite evening going-out clothes: jeans and a T-shirt with "Give Me Coffee and No One Gets Hurt" on the front. I like to warn people how to deal with me in advance. I checked the cover to see what had her so engrossed. It was one of the recent female empowerment books on finding your true self. "Hey, I loved that book."

Evie started, then closed the book and tucked it into her tote. She stood and glanced over at the Drunken Art Studio down the street. "I'm not good with change, so this whole life makeover has me a little on edge. I know it's the best for me and for Homer, but I liked most of my life in New York."

"Most of?" I hadn't talked to her about what brought her to the total opposite coast yet. I figured she'd tell me when she was ready.

"My husband was a jerk. But he was gone a lot. I didn't realize how much of a jerk he was until he changed jobs and stopped traveling." She shook her head. "Lots of people have it worse than me, so I should just be grateful."

"Just because there is suffering in the world doesn't mean your experiences are null." I nodded toward the shop and we started walking. "My experiences have shown me that I need to talk through things before I can put them behind me. And good news? There are a lot of people in South Cove who will tell you what to do; some even have their counselor's license."

"Girl, you're funny." She bumped her shoulder with mine. "No wonder Sasha talked so highly of you and this place. I thought she'd stay around once she got done with school, but I guess that ship sailed."

"I got that feeling too." We crossed the street after checking for any traffic. It was already dark and most of the traffic now would be from people either coming from or going to the winery or Diamond Lille's for dinner. "Are you going to Olivia's birthday party?"

"Of course! I wouldn't miss it." She glanced over at me. "Do you want me to take something with me?"

"Am I that transparent?"

She laughed. "I told her that no one in their right mind without kids would come to this party, but Sasha wanted to invite the world. She's pretty proud of that little girl. Just wait until Olivia graduates from college. That party will be a week long."

I felt a little better, knowing that Evie understood my lack of excitement about going. "I'm going to call Sasha to let her know, but I'm getting together a book basket for Olivia, so if you'd take that, I'd appreciate it."

"You got it." Evie stopped and looked inside the window of the studio.

Art easels stood on each long table, a clean canvas on each one. Paintings lined the room, apparently the results of other classes. And by the wall, a long table with several bottles of wine and a bucket of beer on ice stood with some appetizers and breadsticks. Several people were already inside and the wine was flowing.

Justin hurried up the sidewalk and stopped next to us. "Why are we out here? Let's go in and get something to drink. I'm really not an artist and I tried to get Amy to bow out of this, but you know our girl."

I took his arm and turned toward Evie. "Justin, have you met our newest CBM family member? This is Evie Marshall."

"We met at the coffee shop last weekend." Justin nodded to Evie and offered his other arm. "Nice to see you again. May I escort you inside?"

Evie turned to look at me. "Is he always this polite?"

I nodded as I stepped closer to the shop. "At least he is around me."

"It's an unfortunate side effect of my upbringing. My mother was Miss Manners." When they reached the door Justin moved ahead and held it open. "After you, ladies."

When we got inside he excused himself to meet up with Amy. Evie took a wineglass Greg had brought over when he saw us enter the room. She pointed to Justin. "He's kidding about his mother, right?"

Giggling, I took my glass from Greg. "I believe so. From what I know, Justin's mom is a Legal Aid attorney in Nebraska."

"Ohio," Greg corrected.

I shook my head. "I'm pretty sure it's Nebraska."

"Bet? Loser gets to clean the bathrooms this week?" Greg sipped his wine, watching me.

I nodded. "Evie, would you go ask Justin where he's from? That way there's no interference with the bet."

"You guys take fighting seriously here." Evie moved toward Justin and Amy.

Watching her leave, Greg put his arm around my waist. "Darling, this isn't fighting. This is flirting."

We moved toward the snack table and I snagged a breadstick from the basket. "Sadie's doing a new line of breads now. Like she had time for anything else. Did you know she and Pastor Bill are talking about marriage?"

"He proposed?" Greg filled a plate with cocktail hot dogs and meatballs.

I filled my plate with rolls, butter, and a slice of vanilla cheesecake before it disappeared. "Not yet, but they're talking about what if."

"They're good together." Greg took my plate and went to a table. "Come over here and let's eat before this thing gets started. I didn't get chicken ordered before I had to leave."

"You should have said something. You could have picked up some food before you came." I didn't like it when Greg didn't eat during the day. It usually happened around murder investigations. "What's got you so worked up you're not eating?"

"Who said I was worked up?" He set down the plates and pulled out a chair for me. "I'm going to run and get a beer. Want one?"

I held up the still-full wineglass. "I'm good."

As he hurried away, I notice his glass was still almost full too. What *was* going on?

"Okay, everyone find a seat. We're all here and it's time to be creative," Meredith called out to the room.

"Okay if we sit by you?" Amy sat next to me, pulling Justin into the seat next to her. "This is going to be so much fun. Do you know what we're painting?"

"Probably a seascape." Greg came back with two bottles of beer and handed one to Justin. "Here, buddy, you looked like you needed this."

They clinked bottles.

I turned around in my chair. "Where's Evie?"

"Darla nabbed her and took her over to the side table. I'm pretty sure she's planning on interviewing her for an article on South Cove's newest resident." Amy sipped her wine. "I don't think she's going to get much. Evie's pretty closemouthed about her past. I'm not even positive where she's from."

"New York," both Justin and I said at the same time.

I felt a jerk as a woman walking behind us grabbed the back of my chair to steady herself. Her eyes were a little bloodshot, and the smell of alcohol swept over me as she started talking. "I love visiting New York. We always stay near Times Square, but it's so crazy busy there. Not like this little town. Steve says New York's a cesspool, but I love the vibe you get in the Theater District. All so creative."

"Come along, Nan. No one wants to hear about how much you love New York City." A man in a polo shirt and tan Dockers took the woman by the arm. "Sorry for the bother."

"I didn't bother them," Nan said as he walked her to the last two empty chairs. "They were the ones to bring up New York, not me. Besides, I rarely get to talk to people in person. Video chat only goes so far when you're trying to make a connection. I've told you that time and time again."

When they got seated Meredith tried to get everyone's attention again. "We're going to start painting now. Neal will be walking around and will help if anyone needs refreshments or with paints. I'll be leading you through the class. Make sure you raise your hands high if you don't understand one of my instructions. Art is one percent inspiration and ninety-nine percent perception, so I'm going to teach you perception tonight. The inspiration you can do on your own time."

As we started painting, I leaned toward Greg. "We might as well be doing paint by numbers if we can't be creative."

"Maybe your flower will actually look like a flower this way." He tried to put a dot of paint on my nose. "Stop being such a tortured artist and just follow directions. This is fun."

The evening passed with step-by-step instructions on how to paint the picture. I wasn't sure what we were even painting. I hated not being able to see the big picture. I wanted to copy a painting, not listen to someone tell me to paint five inches of blue across the canvas six inches up from the bottom. How was that going to teach me how to paint?

"I want another drink," I heard Nan say very loudly to her husband when we were on a quick break.

"Drink the water I brought you so you can walk out of here rather than me having to carry you to the car," Steve responded.

I tried not to turn my head to look, but I could feel Greg casually watching the scene to make sure it didn't go south on us. That's one of the problems with living with a guy who works in law enforcement. Constant vigilance is his life. I saw him turn and meet Justin's gaze. The soft jerk of his head in a negative gesture made Justin lean back a bit. Apparently, Greg had backup if he needed it. He just didn't need it quite yet.

I saw Neal walk over and squat between Nan and Steve's chairs. The three of them chatted for a minute, then he got up and moved toward us.

"Can I get you another drink? Maybe a slice of cheesecake?" Neal asked as he paused at our table.

I nodded to the other couple. "Everything okay over there?"

He glanced back at them and sighed. "It's fine. They're just dealing with something no one should need to deal with. It's hard to see them suffering."

"You know them?" Greg's question sounded casual.

Neal shrugged. "Not very well. They're Steve and Nan Gunter. He's some big computer guy over in the valley. She runs a home business. They were at the winery last night and we got to talking. They lost their son a few years ago in a skiing accident. They're still not healed."

"That's so sad." I snuck a peek at Nan and Steve, but they were talking quietly with their heads tilted together. "I don't need anything else, but thank you."

"No problem." His gaze darted up to his wife where she was talking with Darla about her painting. His next words came out tight and forced. "That's what I'm here for, to lend a helping hand."

After he'd left Amy and Justin started talking about wedding plans. No wonder their wedding changed day after day; they were both trying to host a perfect wedding. For everyone who remembered their own wedding day. Helping plan Amy's was part of remembering that day. And the vows everyone took to be man and wife.

I got up and excused myself. I needed to find a bathroom. I followed the signage and found a hallway leading into a dark room. On one side was a restroom with a female picture on the door. She was holding a paintbrush and wore a short smock over nothing else. On the other side of the hall was a bodybuilder guy with the tiniest Speedo on earth covering his private parts. I'd blame the previous owners, but this place had been a high-end pet store before the paint and sip.

Coming out of the bathroom, I saw Justin leaning against the wall. I pointed to the almost naked male form on the door. "It must be a popular place."

Justin looked at the door as if he hadn't seen the painting, and in the dim light, I thought I saw a blush on his face. "Actually, I wanted to talk to you. You're Amy's best friend."

"For many years now. Or at least after you." I wasn't sure I liked where this was going. "What's bothering you?"

"I'm trying to nail down the honeymoon and I want it to be special. Something she'll remember for the rest of her life. But I'm not very good at this stuff." He shuffled his feet and glanced back at the larger room where the others were sitting. "Do you think I could pick your brain in the next few days? I don't want you to plan it or anything, I just want to hear about what you know about Amy. That might spark something."

"Sure. I work most mornings, so if I'm not at the store I'm either home or running Emma. Just stop by or give me a quick text. I could meet you out of town too, if you didn't want Amy to know." I put my hand on his arm. "Although she's going to love anything you decide to do because she loves you."

He nodded and took a deep breath. "That's why I like talking with you, Jill. You make it seem like everything is going to be fine."

"Because it is. This is a wedding. It's only one day, or one week, if you're thinking about the honeymoon, out of your lives. Relax and celebrate." I nodded toward the painting room. "Shall we go back to finish our paintings?"

"Actually, I need to make a stop." He nodded to the door, and this time he did blush. "Who paints their doors like this?"

As I walked back to Greg, I chuckled at Justin's obvious discomfort. He was a good man. And a good match for my over-the-top friend.

Glancing around the main room, I realized Neal was no longer around. Maybe he'd taken the time to make a run for more supplies. I wasn't the only one who'd noticed his disappearance. Meredith was searching the room as well. When she met my gaze she smiled, and her face changed. "Looks like it's time to finish up this masterpiece. Neal had to leave for a few minutes, so if anyone needs anything, well, you're on your own."

"Our wine bottle is empty." Nan stood, weaved, and then moved to the snack table. "Never mind, I found another one."

Chuckles filled the room, but when I looked at Greg, he wasn't smiling. I tried to keep the conversation light. "I hope they're not going to drive out of here."

"Change that sentence to they aren't driving anywhere. I'm not going to allow it. And if they fight me, well, Toby will just get a call as soon as he gets behind the wheel. We might have to make a detour on the way home to drop off those two if no one else is going that way. I'm not taking a chance that he's any more sober that she is." Greg added green to his painting but moved the easel a bit so he could watch Nan and Steve. "This is why I hated my job as a bouncer in college. Some people just don't know their limits."

"I didn't know you had been a bouncer." Amy leaned around me to look at Greg. "So that was your first job in the security field?"

"Bouncing's more like being a childcare worker or a high school playground guard. Someone's always pushing buttons," he grumbled.

"Leave Greg alone, dear. He's in cop mode." Justin nodded at Greg. "If you need help getting them somewhere, we're heading north to my apartment. I can take them if they live that way."

"I'm pretty sure they're tourists. Meredith said they were staying at Main Street B and B."

I glanced over to see where Meredith was. Maybe she could help me with the whole blue section that somehow looked green on my canvas. She was talking to Nan. Hopefully she was having as much of a problem following the directions as I was, because my friends' paintings all looked like the sample in the front of the room. Mine, not so much.

I added white paint to my brush, then swept it over the painting, and for a second I did see the seagulls that we were copying. Then I added more paint and the birds turned into a blob. I dropped my brush onto the butcher paper covering the table. "I hate arts and crafts."

"Jill, don't say that. Your painting is …" Meredith stepped up behind me and studied the mess in front of her. "Well, your painting is original. Can you answer a question? What instruction step didn't you understand? Clearly I'm not giving good directions."

Amy laughed and refilled her wineglass. "I think the more likely answer is Jill's mind was somewhere else and she missed one or two steps in the process. She's always lost in some story or the other."

"That's not fair." I frowned and compared my picture with Greg's and Amy's. Mine didn't look anything like either one of them. I set down my paintbrush and finished off my cheesecake. "I quit. This is just not my jam."

"Never say quit." Meredith started to move on to Greg's picture but stopped. She turned back to me. "But if you wanted to work on it, I have some space in my private lesson schedule. It's a reasonable price and you'll get at least one frameable picture out of the six-week session."

"I think you're misjudging Jill's talent. It might take a little longer than six weeks," Amy responded.

Meredith blushed, staring at my painting. "I'm sure no one could still be this bad after a few intensive lessons. Could they?"

My friends broke out in laughter. I wanted to kick all of them under the table, but I could only reach Greg. What can I say? Love hurts.

"Meredith? Could you help me with something?" Evie called out, and our hostess hurried over and away from me.

Greg leaned up against me. "At least you tried. There's no winner or loser here. It's all about the experience."

"Thanks." I glanced at Greg's picture and tried to copy it. I wanted at least to have something I could hang in my office at the house. Although it might be Greg's version of the seascape that made the final cut. "Miss Emily made this all look easy. Some of her stuff is so beautiful and I can't even paint the ocean."

"Your friend spent many days in her studio before she died. You've been painting all of two hours?" Greg checked his watch. "If we kick Toby out of the apartment, I'll make you an art studio in there."

"As long as you get your workout room, right?" The shed Miss Emily had used as an art studio had been turned into an apartment for Toby when he'd needed a place to live. I kind of liked having him around, especially before Greg had moved in, just to have a guy around. My house is right near Highway 1 and there can be a lot of traffic going down the road. Now that Greg and I were serious, he'd talked several times about changing the apartment into a workout area. He'd even priced out the cost of a sauna to be added near the small bathroom. "Toby hasn't said he's moving yet."

"You're the landlord. Kick his butt out." Greg sat back and contemplated his work.

"Okay, so when he has to quit both the police force and the coffee shop because he can't afford anything nearby, who's going to hire me a new part-time barista?" I sighed and set down my brush. I was done. There was nothing I could do to make this actually look like an ocean. Right now, it looked more like a portrait of The Blob from the movies.

Greg's eyes widened. "Point taken. Speaking of, I need to make sure these guys have a designated driver before they slip out on me."

I watched as Greg went over and introduced himself. I could see the idea of not driving back to the bed and breakfast wasn't going over well, but then Neal came in from outside and joined the discussion. I couldn't hear what was going on, but soon Greg came back to sit by me.

"What's the plan?" I whispered, keeping my gaze away from Steve and Nan.

Greg held out his hand to help me from my chair. "If you're ready, we can head home. Neal's talked them into letting him drive them back. He explained it was all about his insurance, and that if something happened, even a fender bender, he'd be liable. So they agreed to let him drive them back to the B and B."

And just like that, a possible tragedy had been averted.

Chapter 4

Greg's cell rang way too early. He reached over to the nightstand, answered it, and like the perfect gentleman he was, took the call out into the hallway. Or maybe downstairs, as I heard Emma going down, probably wanting out.

I glanced at the clock. Three a.m.! I'm an early riser, but this was ridiculous. I rolled away from the light and went back to sleep.

When my alarm went off I reached over and found Greg's side of the bed cold. Either he hadn't come back to bed or he'd already gotten up and was downstairs drinking coffee. I rubbed my bleary eyes and then rubbed Emma's head as I slipped on my flip-flops. "Hey, girl, do you need to go out? Isn't Greg downstairs?"

That question got a responding woof, which I took to mean that Greg, like Elvis, had left the building. I'd call him later. I went through my morning routine and when I got downstairs I checked the weather. Emma and I would run this afternoon. I had time now, but it was still a little chilly this morning. Besides, the beach looked a little creepy as the fog settled around rock formations and the shore. I liked my run bright and shiny so I didn't run into anything. Or anyone.

I sat down with my coffee and a banana muffin I'd brought home from the shop. Well, I'd brought home an assortment on Monday, but that was just because they hadn't sold over the weekend. Technically, I was doing the shop a favor. I dialed Greg's number. It went straight to voice mail. "Hey, just thinking about you. Call me and tell me what was so important you had to leave our bed at three in the morning."

I hung up, certain I'd thrown just enough guilt into the question so he'd feel obligated to answer. I hated to do it, but a girl's got to have some tricks up her sleeve. I finished my breakfast and took the extra time to read a little in the new romance. I set an alarm to go off just before the shop opened, just in case I'd gotten lost in the story. I'd been right. And when the alarm sounded my head was running with some new book boyfriend who enjoyed long walks on the beach and blowing things up. In a totally good way.

I gave my dog a kiss and started walking into town. Esmeralda's house was dark. She'd probably already left for work an hour ago. I had planned on talking to Greg about how weird she'd been last night, but we'd gotten sidetracked when we arrived home. My cheeks flushed at the memory. And then cooled off right away when I crested the hill and saw the emergency lights ahead. Right in front of the Drunken Art Studio.

Police cruisers and an ambulance were parked in front of the building, lights flashing, but no one except Meredith stood outside the front door. She was staring inside one of the large windows and didn't see me approach. I reached out my hand to touch her arm and she jumped.

"Sorry, I didn't mean to scare you." I glanced around at the empty street. "What happened? Is Neal all right?"

"Besides being a lying cheat?" Meredith shook her head. "Yes, I mean, I guess I don't know. He didn't come home last night. We got in a stupid fight about me treating him like a servant. He has an art degree too. He does digital stuff. It's amazing, just not very popular or accessible for most people. That's why I teach the classes. I'm better with humans. I'm so glad I have a kickboxing class later to wear off all this negativity. I really need to beat on something."

I decided to try a different question. "So, it's not Neal? Why are the police here? And the ambulance? Did you report him in as a missing person?"

"Neal? No, he'll come home. He always does. I'm sure he picked up someone at the bar and went home with her. It's his way of teaching me a lesson. Teaching me who's in charge in our relationship." She rubbed at her face, but I wasn't sure she even realized she was crying.

Okay, so now I knew more about Meredith and Neal's relationship than I wanted to know about anyone's. Ever. I needed to get her focused. Maybe she was in shock. If I could find Greg or Toby or Tim—someone—I could tell them I was taking her over to the shop to get some coffee. But until then, I'd wait with her. Someone should come outside soon. I felt for my phone in my pocket. Maybe I should try to call Greg again. I guess the other question I'd asked Meredith must have sunk in because she turned to look at me.

"Oh my God, Jill. Someone's dead in my shop!" Then her entire body started to shake.

There was a bench outside the building and I led her there and forced her to sit. I sat next to her and grabbed both her hands in mine. They were chilled. "You're cold. Maybe I should take you to the shop. I can just pop in and tell Greg where you'll be. I'll just be a moment."

She reached out with her hands and enclosed mine. "It was the tourist. Nan. She's just lying there, dead. Don't go inside."

I nodded and peeled her hands away from mine. "I need to go open the coffee shop. I'll just call Greg over to the door so I can tell him where you'll be. Do you want some coffee? Or a nice tea? Something warm?"

Meredith took a deep breath and nodded. "Yes, something warm. That would be good. You won't go inside, right? No one should have to see that."

I patted her arm. "I promise, I'll stay right by the door."

When I approached the door I wondered if I'd be able to keep that promise. The building had three steps up out of the doorway to the main floor. As long as they were close, Greg or someone on his team would hear me. But if they were farther into the building I might have to go track them down. I opened the door and ran straight into Toby, who had been coming outside.

"Jill, what are you doing here?" He looked down on me and moved me back outside the doorway. "You can't go inside. It's a mess and I'm not sure how the crime scene guys are going to deal with all the trace they have now."

"Sorry, I just wanted to see if it was okay to take Meredith over to the coffee shop. I need to open and I don't really want to leave her sitting out here alone." I pointed toward the bench, then dropped my arm. It was empty. I glanced around the street. "She was just here."

"I believe you. In fact, Greg told me to take her to the apartment and watch her while he and Tim secured the scene." He scanned the area and stepped around the ambulance to see if she was just on the other side, but no luck.

"Look, if you see her, call me. I've got to go tell Greg she's vanished." Toby blew out a breath. "Some people are just crazy, you know?"

"She said it was one of the people from our class yesterday. I think her name was Nan, and she and her husband, Steve, were staying at Bill and Mary's place. They were both trashed. Maybe she fell and hit her head?" I didn't think Toby would tell me much, but if he nodded at the right places, I'd know if my theory was right.

"Go open the café." Toby shook my shoulder a bit. "And stop trying to trick me out of information. If Greg wants you to know, he can tell you."

"I'll bring over coffee as soon as I get set up." I was going to be the bigger person in this situation. And if I happened to overhear or see something, that wasn't my fault.

"That would be nice." Toby turned and went back inside, and for a second, I felt bad for using coffee to gather information.

Then I saw a woman standing outside the police station a few doors down. I stepped closer and called out, "Meredith?"

The woman's dark hair bounced as she turned and sprinted toward the station door. It hadn't been Meredith. It had been Esmeralda, watching the spectacle. She was probably embarrassed that someone caught her rubbernecking. But honestly, I was surprised that most of South Cove wasn't already out and about trying to find out what happened. South Cove is a very, very small town. It was still early, though.

I crossed the street and went to open my shop. We'd be filled with townsfolk trying to find out what had happened at the newest business in town. Tragedy was good for business. Which was a horrible and jaded thought. But true, nevertheless.

Before I could get over to the art studio with the coffee, Greg came into the shop. He waited for me to finish up what was probably my last commuter and then leaned on the counter. "Good morning, beautiful."

"Hey, hot stuff." I nodded toward the commotion. "You've got the town in an uproar. I've had twice the visitors this morning than normal and everyone asks me what's going on."

"I'm sure you tell them you have no idea, right?" He grinned at me. "Toby said you ran off Meredith."

"I did no such thing. I was going to bring her over to the shop, but I didn't want to take her if you didn't know where she was going." I responded quickly, then saw the grin on Greg's face. "Stop teasing me. Did you find her?"

"Yeah, she'd gone back up to the apartment to get her cell phone and to see if Neal had come back yet." Greg shook his head. "All I can say is those two have marital issues that are extreme enough to get them on one of those talk shows."

"I heard part of it." I shook my head. "Some people shouldn't be together. It's more of a power play relationship than a supportive one. There's no way I'd put up with it."

He nodded. "Anyway, Toby said you volunteered coffee?" He started stacking paper cups. "I think I need enough for four, maybe five. The EMTs left about thirty minutes ago when Doc showed up with his own help."

"Doc Ames is here?" My shoulders sagged. "So she's dead?"

"I think you already knew that, but yeah. The victim was that drunk woman from the class. I don't know why she was in the building, but according to Meredith the door might have been unlocked when she came down. I guess she thought Neal was going to lock it. And Neal didn't." He rubbed his hand through his hair. "And again, thank you for making our relationship normal and sane."

"That takes two." I handed him two carafes of coffee, then bagged up a dozen assorted treats from the dessert case that would travel across the street well. Which meant cookies and chocolate-filled croissants. And a few muffins. "Let me know if you need more coffee. Toby can bring the carafes back if he's working today. Or do I need to switch his schedule?"

"He's already called Deek and they switched out. I was supposed to mention that too." He glanced at his phone when a text beeped. "That's Bill. The husband is awake and eating breakfast."

"Did he notice his wife was even gone?" I made a note to charge the food off to our Jill account and then watched Greg's reaction.

"According to Bill's text, when he asked about the Mrs., the guy said she liked taking morning walks and would be back soon to eat. Steve asked if he needed to call her to get her back at a specific time." Greg shook his head. "Bill could be an actor, he played that so well. I called him and asked him to let me know when the guy came down. I'm heading over there now, as soon as I drop off the food for the guys. Thanks, Jill."

He leaned in for a kiss, then snuck a croissant from the bag. "I guess I need to eat and run. See you when I see you."

Which meant he probably wouldn't be home except to sleep and shower. Murder investigations were hard on Greg. He didn't like the thought of anyone dying in our quiet town. And definitely not being murdered.

As if they'd been waiting for Greg to leave, a pile of customers flooded into the shop. Some went over to browse the bookcases as they watched out the windows to see what Greg did now. Others came up to order coffee and a treat. The good thing was, there were too many of them for me to have time to chat. Which meant I could avoid any pointed questions.

Evie came down at eight to grab coffee. She had on sweats and a jacket and Homer curled in one arm. I leaned in for doggy kisses as she filled a travel mug with coffee. "Is it always this busy on your shift? The last few days I've come down, it's been dead in here."

"No, we have lookie-loos from the incident." I lowered my voice. "You're going to hear it sooner rather than later, so here you go. The drunk woman last night at the paint thing? The tourist with her husband? She was killed this morning."

Evie's eyes widened. "By whom? Her husband? He didn't seem that mad at her."

I shrugged. "I don't know. But you need to know because people are going to ask you what you know during your shift. Deek's coming in instead of Toby, so he'll help divert any questions, but you don't know anything."

"I don't know anything," Evie explained.

I nodded. "Exactly."

"No, I mean I *don't* know anything. Why would they ask me?" Evie looked totally confused. Homer kept watching her face, wondering if his walk had just been sidelined.

"Because you work here. Because I'm dating Greg. Well, we're living together." I shrugged. "It's just always been that way. People think we're in the know on all kinds of things, when usually I'm the last to know something. Maybe it's the fact we're a coffee shop. Like the old general stores in the past, with a stove for the old guys to sit and talk around?"

"Okay, not what I expected, but I can play dumb." She glanced over toward the Drunken Artist. "That poor woman. I feel so bad for her."

"Me too." I watched as Evie took her coffee and her dog to the back room and the back door. I liked having Homer around. His bright eyes took in everything and everyone and he seemed to love his new home. Evie—she was a little harder to read. But she worked hard and people liked her. I just hoped she liked being here as much as Homer seemed to like the California coast.

I refilled the dessert case in between helping customers. Deek came in a couple of hours before his shift started. He had his laptop bag on his shoulder. He glanced around the still-crowded shop and came around the counter. "I came in to write before my shift, but if you need help…"

"No worries. I'm handling it. Besides, it's been a while since I've had a busy shift. I didn't even have time to read today." I nodded to the last piece of caramel-drizzled cheesecake on the cardboard on the back counter. "That one's too broken to put on sale. Do you want it?"

"Sure. Unless you do." Deek knew my sweet tooth.

I shrugged. "I've already destroyed a piece so I could call it damaged. And ate it."

"Your aunt would go nuts if she heard you say that." Deek winked at me, dished up the cheesecake, and went to find an empty table.

As if he'd called her into being by mentioning her name, my aunt came into the shop. She wore a cashmere sweater set, pants, and a string of pearls. Her Wednesday casual. She froze a minute as she took in the busy shop. Then she came around the corner and put on an apron. "If you needed help, you should have called. I would have worn something I didn't have to dry-clean. My plan was just to go over the books this morning."

I took away the apron from her and shooed her into the back room. "I don't need help. And if I do, Deek's over there in the corner. I'll ask him to start early."

Deek waved at my aunt, who nodded at him. Then she glanced around the still-crowded room. "Are you sure?"

"Positive." I wanted to roll my eyes. Apparently, no one thought I was able to run my own shop when I had a few more customers than normal. It was beginning to give me a complex.

Aunt Jackie nodded, then moved to the back. "I'll be back here, then."

When my shift finally ended I was more than ready to hand over the reins. Deek came over and put away his tote bag. "I finished a chapter and started a new one. Great writing day for me. How'd you do?"

"There are still tables to clean, I'm behind on dishes, and my feet hurt." I leaned against the counter and slipped off my apron to toss into the laundry bin. "But I'll leave that to you. I'm heading to Diamond Lille's for lunch."

"Greg meeting you?"

I shook my head and held up the romance I'd had tucked in my tote since the shift started. "Nope. I'm sharing my meal with a handsome and charming bad-boy book boyfriend."

Chapter 5

Diamond Lille's best waitress—okay, fine, she could be the best in the freaking world—Carrie saw me come in the door. "I've got your favorite booth ready for you. Anyone joining you?"

Apparently, everyone thought I needed a dining companion. I must be hungry. I was second-guessing everything anyone said to me. Instead of reacting, I smiled as I patted my tote. "Just me and a book today."

She held up a menu. "Do you need this or are you getting fish and chips?"

"And a vanilla shake." I waved away the menu as I walked to the booth. I didn't like having too many choices. Besides, when you find a meal you love, you should just accept it. Trying new things just made you wish you'd stuck with your original order.

Which apparently was my motto for dating and relationships too. People like Neal went through trial after trial but still kept coming back to the one he'd married. Was it because of the commitment? Or did he love Meredith in some twisted way?

I took a deep breath. I didn't want to think about Meredith and Neal anymore. I wanted to read a book with a relationship I knew would be fine at the end. There might be ups and downs and a big, black moment. But there would also be fun and games and hope that everything could turn out.

I needed some positive and happy in my life today.

I pulled out my book and saw Esmeralda pass by my booth and head for the door.

"Esmeralda?"

Either she hadn't heard me or she was ignoring me. I set down the book and moved to stand so I could catch her, but just then Carrie arrived with the shake.

She saw my movements and glanced behind her. When she didn't see anything wrong, like a band of gun-toting nuns coming toward us, she turned back to me. "Everything all right, dear?"

"Yeah, I just thought I saw Esmeralda."

Carrie nodded. "She came in to eat after her shift ended at about eleven. The poor girl looks so tired. Running two jobs is hard on those of us approaching middle age."

I leaned back in my seat. What was I going to do? Run Esmeralda down and demand to know why she was avoiding me? Especially when I'd just seen her last night? "You're as young as you feel."

Carrie chuckled. "That's a lie they tell us so we'll feel better."

As she walked away, I wondered if she'd known Doc had been in town this morning. I suspected she and our county coroner talked a lot, and often. Especially from the blush that had crawled up both their faces when I'd asked each of them separately if they were dating yet. It was hell living in a small town when you were trying to hide a secret.

I picked up the book and got lost in the story. My favorite pastime.

* * * *

The afternoon passed slowly. Nothing out of the ordinary happened. Emma and I ran on an almost empty beach. I love March. I thought about stopping to chat with Esmeralda, but she had a car at her house and I didn't want to interrupt a reading. Even if I didn't truly believe in her gift, others did, and paid big bucks for her counsel. I wondered, because the Gunters had lost a child, if they'd been in town to talk with our resident fortune-teller. Esmeralda should have told them to avoid the art studio if they had talked to her. But maybe these glimpses into the future or talks to the dead didn't work that way.

All I knew was my future was in my own hands. I was a big fan of the motto, *If it's going to be, it's up to me.* And as I looked around my cluttered living room, I realized the saying should be on the top of my cleaning list this afternoon. I glanced at the book I'd pulled out of my tote before I ran but turned away from it. It was my month to clean the house and I'd put it off long enough.

I'd just finished the downstairs when my stomach growled. I glanced at the clock. It was already almost seven. Greg hadn't called, but with an active investigation, that wasn't unusual. I hoped that Nan Gunter had gone back to the studio after realizing she'd left something there and had some kind of accident. Dying from an accident while you're on vacation was tragic enough. Being murdered just didn't seem fair. And if it *was* an accident, the case would be closed quickly and life in South Cove would go on. Well, for some of us. I figured Meredith and Neal needed to use the unfortunate incident to get their crap together or figure out that their marriage wasn't working. Leaving the door to the studio open hadn't caused Nan's death, but it had made it easy for her to fall there. I pushed the thoughts out of my head. Not my place to judge someone else's relationship. Especially people I didn't know well, like the new business owners. But if this behavior continued, I was afraid they wouldn't make friends in South Cove very easily. We were a tight-knit group and we were always in one another's business.

That got me thinking of Justin and his honeymoon plans. Amy had mentioned that she'd always wanted to visit Alaska. Maybe that would be in Justin's budget. They liked hiking almost as much as they liked surfing. But would Alaska be too cold for a spring getaway? Maybe I should think of more southern destinations. As I made dinner, I also made him a list of places I knew Amy had talked about visiting someday. As I ate my ham sandwich and small salad for dinner, I put all the ideas into an email and sent it to his work address.

When I got a quick email back with "Thanks" as the one-word response, I figured my work was done. I cleaned up the kitchen, let Emma out and back in, then took my dog and my book upstairs to read in bed.

The next morning my alarm woke me. Greg's side of the bed was empty. He hadn't come home last night. Which meant one thing: Nan hadn't just slipped and fallen. She'd probably been murdered. I got ready for my day. The shop was going to be busy again, or would be as soon as the news got out. And my first customer would probably be Darla. Not only was she our city's unofficial marketing queen and ran the winery, she also wrote for the *South Cove Gazette*. And this was just the type of story she loved getting her teeth into.

Emma watched me as I finished preparing to leave. Then she made three circles in her dog bed and plopped down with a big sigh. Her gaze never left the leash hanging by the door. I knelt down and gave her a hug. "You know we'll go this afternoon. As soon as it warms up, we'll start running in the morning again. Then you'll be wanting an afternoon run instead. You know you're spoiled, right?"

She just closed her eyes and ignored that comment. Emma knew she was loved. By more people than just me and Greg. Toby thought she was part his dog too. Maybe as one of the privileges of renting my cottage.

The good news was, I always had someone to pet sit when Greg and I went out of town.

The Drunken Artist still had police tape blocking the door. Another bad sign for this event being an accident. And when I reached Coffee, Books, and More, my hunch became official. Darla waited for me on one of the small outdoor tables in front of the shop. She was writing in a little notebook that she tucked away when I walked up. "Jill, what do you know about the murder?"

"Good morning, Darla. Lovely day for March, isn't it?" I unlocked the door. "Please come in. Would you like coffee?"

Darla followed me into the shop. "Okay, fine, so I was a little overanxious. My deadline's at noon, and besides the rumors I heard last night at the winery, I've got zero information on this murder."

I went about my opening chores, not saying anything.

She climbed onto one of the stools and got out her notebook. Then she sighed. "Could I have a coffee with just a squeeze of honey? I'm trying to break the sugar habit and I don't want to go with artificial sweeteners."

"Sure. I can do that. Or I could put a pump of French vanilla in it. Same calorie count, but you get the vanilla taste along with the sweetness." I filled a coffee cup with our medium blend. "And much lower in calories than your regular. Sometimes it's the small things we do over and over that make big changes for us."

"Now you sound like Matt." She smiled at his name. She and Matt had been dating for years. He'd become a fixture in South Cove after arriving from a work program that had brought a lot of the businesses' new employees. Including Evie's cousin, Sasha, who'd worked for the bookstore. "He said to tell you hi, by the way. I'm falling down on all my social obligations."

"No worries. Greg and I will have to come by some night once this investigation is over and we can all catch up." I set the coffee in front of her and poured my own cup without any additions. I brought it around the counter and sat next to her. So far the store was quiet, but soon at least my commuters would come in and interrupt us. It was better to get the conversation over with.

"You're telling me there is an investigation." Darla's eyes sparkled with excitement.

I shrugged in answer. "Maybe. The signs point that way. But I haven't seen much of Greg since three yesterday morning, so I can't give you any particulars. When he came for coffee yesterday he didn't know anything yet. And that was the last time I saw him."

Darla set down her pen and picked up her coffee. She gave it a sip and her eyes widened in surprise. "This is good."

"I know."

She took another sip, then set the cup down. "It was that Nan woman from the painting class who's dead. Correct?"

Greg didn't like me sharing information he'd given me, but he hadn't given me anything, so I guessed I could play Clue with Darla without any guilt. But I wasn't talking about Meredith and Neal's relationship. That wasn't my story. Not at all. "Yeah. Nan Gunter. Neal met her and her husband the night before, at your winery. Maybe you saw them there?"

Darla shook her head. "I hadn't seen them before. Of course, Monday's my night off, so I wasn't at the winery. I'll have to talk to Robin. She bartends on Monday nights. It's always a small crowd, so once the kitchen staff have left, she would have been all by herself. Thanks for that lead anyway."

"No problem. That's about all I know. Neal might be able to tell you more." *If he was home*, I added silently.

"I didn't pay much attention to them at the painting night. I was more interested in talking to your new barista. Evie's so fascinating. Did you know she wrote grant proposals for a women's shelter in New York for a while?"

I did, but I'd also known she'd stayed at that shelter for a couple of weeks. That wasn't my story to tell. "She's had an interesting life."

Darla paused, looking at me for a minute as if she could read my thoughts or something. But then she put it away. I could see the idea dive back behind her eyes and hover there for another time. "She sure has. I saw her walking her dog the other day. He's so cute."

"If I thought Emma wouldn't sit on it, I'd get a pom puppy in a heartbeat." I could feed my yearning by playing with Homer, though. And that was almost as good.

"I know you're holding out on me, but I'm not sure if it's the murder case or Evie." Darla held up her hand when I started to tell her I didn't know what she meant. "Don't lie to me. I'll let you have your secret for now. But someday I'm going to ask you to tell me the truth and you're going to need to tell me. Because we're friends."

Now I felt like a complete jerk. Was there anything else I could tell her about Nan's death? I shook my head and held up my arms. "Honestly, I think your best bet is to talk to Neal and your bartender. You'll probably get way more from them than anything I could tell you. I only met them last night, and it really wasn't a true meeting."

Darla put away her notebook and sipped her coffee. "What else is going on in South Cove? I hear our friend Sadie and the pastor are getting very chummy."

That made me grin. "I see wedding bells in the future for those two. It's time for Sadie to have someone in her life again. Nick's all grown and almost out of college. He's going into finance and will be amazing. Was Pastor Bill ever married?"

"Yes, to his high school sweetheart. She died young. In childbirth, I believe. Her *and* the baby. It was all so sad. He was new to town. South Cove was his first assignment after seminary. Then tragedy struck. It's nice to see him happy again." Darla finished her coffee and slipped off her stool. "I guess I'd better go run down these leads. Thanks for chatting with me. What do I owe you for the coffee?"

"It's free. We're friends." I shooed her out the door and watched her leave to go talk to Meredith and Neal. I wondered if they had their happy masks back on or if I should have sent her somewhere else. Somewhere safe.

Chapter 6

Toby arrived just before his shift was set to start. His eyes were already drooping. He grabbed a cup and put ice in it, then filled it with coffee. After he drank the contents he slipped on an apron and leaned against the counter. "Hey, boss."

"Are you sure you can handle this?" I took in his rumpled shirt and less-than-perfect hair. "I can stay and work until Aunt Jackie's shift starts. I'll have Evie to help."

"And so will I. Honestly, I need the money. I'm really close to having twenty percent to put down, but every time I get close, prices rise and I need more. But I'm determined. And I have my eye on a little cottage outside Bakerstown that my Realtor says is coming on the market soon." He sighed. "I could just get a bigger loan, but I hate to pay that loan insurance, PMI, if I don't have to."

"You're a hard worker. You'll figure it out." I hesitated.

Toby must have read my mind. "And before you offer, I don't need a bridge loan from the Miss Emily fund. At least not yet. If this house comes on the market before I'm ready, I'll come with my hat in hand."

"It's not like that." I smiled as he filled another cup with hot coffee this time. "It's just the money's just sitting there."

"It's your money. But I appreciate the offer. And like I said, this house is the one I want. It's in a good school district, just in case. It has a fenced yard, so Emma can visit. And from what I've seen on the outside, it feels right. Now it just has to come in at the right price." He waved to a customer who came in and zoomed over to the mystery section. "Anyway, I'm here. You can go home."

I took off my apron and paused. "Have you heard anything about Nan's death?"

"Yes, I have." He turned to empty the dishwasher.

"You're a brat." I picked up my tote and headed out the door. "I'll be at Lille's, then running, then home if anyone's looking for me."

"I think we can get by one shift without asking you any questions." He waved at her. "Go on. Have a great lunch."

"Greg's probably not coming home for dinner, so eating a big lunch is easier, then I can just heat up soup for dinner." I held the door handle as I explained my choices.

"Whatever makes you feel better about it." He grinned.

Toby was a good guy. He deserved to find the one and settle down not only with a house but with a wife and a family. I hoped the house was just the first step in his future. I stepped away and realized I hadn't told Toby about Olivia's birthday party yet. It really wasn't my place to tell him that Sasha was in a new relationship, but if I told him about the party, I'd have to tell him that too. I wouldn't want him to go to the party blind.

I hurried past Antiques by Thomas and hoped Josh wouldn't see me walk by. I must have been under a lucky star for at least today because I got by and all the way to Diamond Lille's before I saw anyone I knew.

When I walked in Amy was sitting in one of the booths. She waved me over. "Hey, I should have called you. Justin was supposed to meet me for lunch, but I just got a text he's tied up."

"Well, this really is my lucky day, then." I got settled into the booth and hoped we'd be able to talk about anything but Amy's upcoming wedding. The girl was obsessed and she still had a month to go. They'd had to put it off once already due to Justin's family having issues getting out to California last month, so now the date was set for the first weekend in April. If they had to put it off any longer, I think Amy was going to explode with wedding jitters. "Have you ordered yet?"

"I was waiting for Justin, so no. But we can now." She waved Carrie over. "I have a new lunch companion."

"Well, isn't this lovely. I don't think I've seen the two of you for a weekday lunch for months now." Carrie glanced at me. "Do you want a menu today?"

I nodded. "I need something that's going to hold me over until dinner. Greg's probably going to be stuck at the station."

She handed me a menu she'd had tucked under her arm. "Are you up for shakes today or iced tea?"

"Iced tea," Amy said. "I gained two pounds last month due to this wedding stress. I need to fit into my dress in a few weeks."

"Same for me." I also had to fit into a maid of honor dress, but I hadn't ordered a size smaller than the one I normally wore like my friend had. The crazy thing was she could skip eating a candy bar for breaks and she'd lose the weight. I'd have to starve to drop a size in a month. But I could support her by not having a creamy shake in front of her. "What's going on with Justin? Work keeping him busy?"

"That's what he says, but I don't know. Maybe I've finally driven him away with all this wedding mania. He told me to stop talking about the flatware last night. He said no more wedding planning. 'What we have is what we're doing.' And if people can't show up? Apparently, that's their problem." Amy brushed back her hair with one hand. "Can you believe it? I think he means it too. He's mad at his family."

"They did pull up short last month. They should have known this was going to be an issue long before it was. Hopefully adding a month is enough for them." I studied the menu like I hadn't seen it twice or more a week for years.

"Justin says they thought he would pay the costs if they bailed. According to him, they're always asking him for money. And not just his brother. I guess his folks do too." Amy set down the menu. "His family makes me glad it's just me and my dad. We might not be much, but we've always been there for each other."

"And when you get married it will be you and Justin. He'll stand for you." I made a decision and set down the menu. "You two are perfect for each other. Family might be what you're born with, but you both have a family you built here in South Cove."

Amy leaned over the table and face hugged me. "You're the best friend a girl could ever have."

"I know." I smiled at her, then waved to Carrie. "Let's get lunch ordered before Mayor Baylor calls to check on his best employee. When are he and Tina getting back from the cruise?"

We ordered lunch and as we waited, Amy's eyes widened. "OMG. Did you hear that Esmeralda put in her two weeks? Is that crazy or what? She needs the health insurance the job provides. We just talked about this a month ago. What is she thinking?"

"I don't know. She came over this week and told me that she's doing it so Greg won't feel conflicted. Do you think she has a crush on him?" I'd waited for Carrie to drop off my chicken Marsala and Amy's salad before.

"Like he'd do it anyway. The guy is madly in love with you." Amy shook her head. "It's not Greg, but I don't know why she's quitting."

I didn't either, but I didn't like it. Esmeralda was too goal-focused to just quit her job on a whim, especially because she needed the health insurance. "Maybe I need to talk to her again."

"Well, you need to do it soon. The mayor will put up the job on the board quicker than we can say 'new employee.' She's paid a really good wage and he can get someone out of college for a lot less to start." Amy glanced at her watch. "And speaking of my boss, I'd better finish up and get back. He wants me to email him the budget this afternoon. I think he's already spending the extra personnel budget before he even gets home from vacation."

I finished my meal and said goodbye to my friend. She was going through a lot right now with the wedding and work. Of course, a lot of her stress she brought on herself, but I still felt bad for her. Amy was my friend, even when she went bridezilla on me. And hopefully this would be the last marriage for her, so I wouldn't have to go through it again. Thinking of late marriages, I dialed my aunt as soon as I arrived home.

Sitting at the table, I put the phone on Speaker and took a soda from the fridge. I heard the click when she answered and hurried back to the table.

"I'm going to be at the shop today at four." My aunt snapped into the phone without giving me the chance to even say hello.

"Good to know. How are you? How's Harrold? How did the trip go?" I peppered her with questions.

"That's why you called? To find out about our vacation?" Her voice sounded confused.

"I haven't talked to you since the staff meeting on Wednesday. I missed you." I leaned against the chair. I'd thrown her off-balance. And I loved it. "Besides, I desperately need a vacation, but unless I go on my own, I'm going to live through you and Harrold's experience. Greg's tied up in a case."

She tapped her fingers on some sort of hard surface. My phone picked up a lot of background noise. I thought there might be a way to filter it, but honestly, I didn't know how. And I didn't have time to track down a teenager to help me.

"Well, I can see your point. But I've got no time to just chat. I'm needed in the store in less than two hours and Harrold and I are just finishing lunch."

"Okay, then I'll call you later," I said, but then I realized she'd already hung up. My aunt was a determined woman and an acquired taste. I guess I just still hadn't gotten used to her communication style. I glanced around the house.

I'd let Emma out when I'd arrived home. I'd cleaned the entire downstairs yesterday. I had two choices: Clean the upstairs, including stripping beds. Or find something else to keep me occupied for a few hours until it was time for me to make dinner.

I figured I needed to go upstairs and clean, but I was holding out for a better option. Emma barked at the back door, and I realized that was my other option. We needed to go for a run.

The day was beautiful, the sky too blue and the ocean a shiny, blue-gray that made me want to cry. I'd run my usual path on the beach and now was walking back to the parking lot. Then I crossed the road that headed up to my house. I had a routine. A family had set their blankets and chairs near the water's edge in front of me. The father wore multicolored swim shorts. The little boy, who must have been three or four, had a matching suit. The mom had a cover-up over her suit, but even with that, I could see the baby bump. A family of three was soon to be one of four. The sight made me smile. Someday I could see Greg and me in that moment.

As I watched, the mom pulled out a full picnic from a bag she'd carried. She laughed when her husband started helping. I guessed he was giving her grief for carrying too much on her own. He touched her face, and then her belly. The action seemed too private for me to intrude upon, even with just my gaze.

Seeing that family and their connection made me want to visit the station and Greg. So I turned toward the parking lot and we started our walk to town. I didn't bring Emma into town a lot but she liked visiting Greg at the station. Esmeralda always kept dog treats for her at her desk. Another thing that would change if she actually quit.

When I got close to the station I noticed a man standing at the police station door. He pounded on the glass door. Emma growled and pulled on the leash. I motioned her to sit and pulled out my phone.

"You witch!" he screamed at the door. "You're the reason she's dead. You probably killed her just so your reading would come true. Come out here and talk to me."

I dialed Greg. There was no way this was going to wind up in just a friendly talk. The guy wanted blood.

He kept hammering while the phone was ringing. When Greg picked up I sighed with relief and sat on a bench to watch the fireworks. I needed to get Emma settled before she did something about the guy yelling.

"Look, Jill, I can't talk right now. I'm in a meeting."

"Have you noticed someone banging on your side door? The employee entrance? He looks like he's trying to break in and look pretty angry." I pulled out my keys. My hands were shaking and it took a few tries to get the door open. I kept the phone between my head and shoulder. "I'm taking Emma home, but you need to get someone out there, fast."

I hurried away pulling Emma behind me and glanced over my shoulder. She wanted to deal with the issue. The man was still there. Still banging.

"Are you all right?" Greg's voice pulled me out of my imaginations "I've got Toby going out there. What's going on?"

"Honestly, I don't know." I hurried down the street. "I think he's yelling at Esmeralda. He's yelling awful things."

"You should go home. I've got to see what's happening. It's a crazy week. I'll call you later."

I sat at the kitchen table with Emma's head in my lap and talked to her about the craziness that had just happened. I heard Greg's truck pull into our driveway, and in a few minutes he was at the back door. He let himself in with his key and then stood and watched me and Emma for a second.

He grabbed a soda out of the fridge and sat down next to me. "It's okay. He didn't get inside and he didn't do any damage."

"What happened? Was he someone off the road? You're always warning me about people from the road. Why was he yelling?" I leaned over closer to him and laid my head on his shoulder. "Who was he yelling at?"

"I take it you didn't recognize him, then." Greg opened his soda and took a sip.

I shook my head. "I know someone that crazy?"

"Kind of. Jill, that's Steve, Nan's husband. He says that Esmeralda was blackmailing them for money. And when Nan wouldn't pay, she killed her."

"That's crazy. What does Esmeralda say?"

He shook his head. "That's just it. She won't talk about it. She just said that this is why she couldn't work for me. Not right now."

"That's not the same as saying she did something wrong," I defended her choice of words.

"And it's not denying the charges either." He sipped his soda again. "Look, I'm going to do everything I can to find out what really happened, but I think you might want to prepare yourself that maybe Esmeralda did have something to do with this death. Maybe it was a spur-of-the-moment reaction or an accident, but there's a lot of evidence that puts her near the victim."

I stared at him, not believing what he was saying. "There was no way Esmeralda could be involved with this. She reveres life. She gets in fights with farmers because they aren't feeding their animals enough. I don't believe it."

Greg didn't look at me for a long time. "I'm not sure I do either."

Chapter 7

Darla was at the coffee shop waiting for me again the next morning. She didn't say anything until I'd set her new favorite in front of her and had come around and sat next to her.

"This can't be true."

I sipped my coffee. I was going to need it because I'd been up most of the night, tossing and turning. "That's what I said."

"She's so granola. She doesn't even kill flies. She traps them and then drives out to the mountains to drop them off." Darla sipped her coffee.

I hadn't known that about Esmeralda, but it didn't surprise me. "Greg doesn't think she did it either."

"That won't help if she won't talk." Darla stabbed at the counter with her finger. "I read a story about a woman who didn't fight her sentence and went to jail for decades even though she didn't do the crime."

"We have to find the real killer." The words were out of my mouth before I could stop them. Greg would be furious with me, but if he thought I was going to let one of my friends go down without a fight, well, he didn't know me very well.

"Hold on a minute." A voice came from the back office. "Before the two of you go all *Thelma and Louise* on me, what are we talking about? Who was murdered?"

Evie came out of the back office holding Homer in her arms. He yipped a quick greeting, his tail wagging furiously when he saw me. What can I say? Dogs love me.

"Look, you probably shouldn't get involved. Greg won't like it." I reached out and rubbed Homer on the chin. "Heck, I shouldn't get involved, but Esmeralda is one of my friends. And you don't turn your back on friends."

"Then I'm in as well." Evie pulled up a chair. "Esmeralda's the police dispatcher who is also a fortune-teller, right? Who is she supposed to have killed?"

Darla caught Evie up on the conversation while I helped a commuter with her morning java hit. When the shop was quiet again I came back to join them.

"The only evidence is this guy throwing a fit at the station? Over some sort of reading?" Evie shook her head. "Isn't that a little weak for evidence?"

"You're right. There must be something else that puts her at the crime scene." Darla pulled out a piece of paper. "I'll go to the station to see what I can learn with my press pass. Jill, you go into Bakerstown and talk to Doc Ames. And maybe over to the Main Street B and B? Bill's still kind of upset over the last article I wrote about the City Council."

"The one where you called them all dinosaurs? And said they were too old to manage the city?" I stared at Darla.

"I was making a point. No one reads the City Council notes anyway." Darla turned red.

"I think Bill might." I looked at Evie. "Do you have plans for your day off? Want to meet some people? You being along will give me an excuse to go visiting."

"Sure! I was just going to unpack a few boxes. This will be more fun." She glanced down at Homer. "I'd better go walk him. He's been so good. I hate to push it."

"No problem. I'll pick you up at one?" I figured it would take me that long to get back to the house and get the Jeep after Deek came for his shift. "Meet me here and we'll walk over to Main Street B and B before we drive into Bakerstown."

"Sounds great. I'm so excited to be part of your squad." Her eyes twinkled as she went out the front door, holding it open for Greg.

Darla saw him coming in and stuffed her notebook into her overflowing tote. "I'm heading over there now. The boys are easier to get information out of than your man is. So keep him here for a while and I'll see what I can find out. I'll call you tonight."

"Thanks, Darla," I picked up the cups and carried them to the sink. When I turned around Greg was standing by the counter, watching me. "Hey, honey, what's going on?"

He glanced at the door through which Darla had just escaped. Then he slipped onto one of the stools. "Just stopped in for some coffee and a chat. What are you doing?"

I didn't like the edge in his voice. He suspected what we'd been talking about and I could tell it. However, there were also other, innocent conversations that could have been happening. I wasn't proud of it, but I went with the lie. I poured him a cup of coffee and set it in front of him. "Darla wanted to be introduced to Evie so she could go over some of the festival plans. Evie's really interested in marketing."

"Really?" Greg sipped his coffee. "I would have thought they knew each other because they sat next to each other at the painting party. Didn't I hear Amy say they met at the Business-to-Business meeting?"

"Well, maybe 'introduce' was the wrong word. Darla wanted to talk to her and she came down with Homer and we all talked." I felt my cheeks burning. I wasn't good at lying.

"Honey, do me a favor and try to stay out of trouble while you're investigating Nan's murder. Please?" He leaned back into his chair.

My first thought was to deny the accusation. He might be trying to trick me. Get me to say I'd be careful but then jump and tell me to stay out of this. I hated reverse psychology. I never knew how to react to it. Especially when someone had caught me in a bald-faced lie. "Look, I don't know what you expect here. There's no way that Esmeralda killed that woman. I'm not going to let her go down for something she didn't do."

"I didn't say you should." He nodded to the brownie in the case. "Do those have walnuts?"

"Yep." I plated the brownie and set it in front of him with a fork. "So, you think I should investigate?"

"I didn't say that either." He took a bite of the brownie. "This is the one thing Sadie makes that could turn me into a stress eater. She's an amazing baker."

"Yes, she is." I thought about getting one for me, but I'd already had a muffin when I arrived at the shop. What could I say? It'd been a stressful day. "We have a plan. If I find something, I'll let you know. How's Esmeralda holding up?"

"That's what bothers me. She's calm; too calm. It's like she knows the community is coming with pitchforks to kill her at any moment." He sighed, then glanced up to see my face. "I can't help her if she won't help herself. She won't even tell me where she was when Nan was killed."

"Maybe she has a secret," I thought, my brain working slower than molasses.

"One that's not about her killing someone? Let's hope so." He finished off his brownie in his second bite. "Can I have a to-go coffee refill? I need to get back on the street. I'm interviewing anyone who was in town that night. Well, we're interviewing them. Toby and Tim already started at the other end of town. I think they went to hit Diamond Lille's so they could order some food. The pair of them have been running since the beginning of the week."

"So have you," I reminded him.

A smile filled his just-a-little-too-broad-to-be-regal face. With the dusting of hair on his cheeks, he made me sigh. It was a good thing he was my boyfriend already.

I shook away the image. It must just be too close to Valentine's. I needed some fresh air. "Anyway, you're not getting any closer to finding the killer standing around here."

"Yeah, but I know you're not out there getting into trouble." He glanced at the door. "I take it Darla was running to the station to try to get one of the guys to talk?"

"She's going to be mad when she realizes they're out canvassing the town." I sipped my coffee. "I'm taking Evie with me so she can meet Doc Ames and Mary and Bill."

"You're a giver, that's what you are." He stood and picked up his coffee. "But actually, knowing you'll have someone with you makes me feel just a little better. Try not to tick off the bad man, okay?"

"You tell me who it is and I'll stay far, far away from them." I leaned in and gave him a quick kiss. "I'd better get some work done. Aunt Jackie's working today and if I don't have my close chores done, she'll notice."

"I think you're more scared of your aunt than meeting up with a possible killer."

I nodded as I took out the close list. "And I think you're very perceptive."

By the time Deek arrived I had all my close chores done and had started on some of his shift tasks. He was going to be alone today and I knew that the shop would be swamped as soon as it got out that Esmeralda was number one on the suspect list. The good news was that people bought a lot of coffee and snacks while they were gossiping. The better news was it wouldn't be during my shift.

He came around the counter, took one look at me, and shook his head. "Uh-oh. You're up to something."

"There is no way you can see that in my aura. Who did you talk to?" My eyes narrowed as I watched his reaction.

He laughed as he put the apron on over his head. "Sorry, Toby told me. I guess Greg told him that you and your new pals were going all private investigator this afternoon and he was to watch over you if he saw you."

"That's a little patronizing if you ask me." I glared at my barista. "And you of all people shouldn't go along with it. Especially when your mom is a strong, independent woman."

"I think the bigger question is are you going to tell her?" He started counting desserts in the case. "I really don't want to have to move before I finish this book and the publisher showers advance money on me."

"You are such a dreamer. And I should tell your mom." I shook a finger at him, which I knew he'd just laugh at. No one on my staff took me the least bit seriously and I loved it that way. "Anyway, if Evie comes down before I get back, tell her to wait for me."

"Yes, ma'am." He glanced at the almost-empty dining room. "You sure you don't want to stay and help with the crowd when it arrives?"

"Nah, you can do it." I swung my tote over my shoulder. "If you need help, you can ask Aunt Jackie to come in early."

"I'll be fine." He glanced at me nervously. "Won't I?"

I shrugged. "Maybe, maybe not."

As I walked home, I thought about the way the crew had turned into more than just a team. We were a family. And I had three brothers along with Greg to tease me. The shop had turned into more than just a way to make enough money to live on. It had become a gathering spot where people came for a minute of silence or to step out of the heat of the day. We were as much of an institution now as Diamond Lille's, even though the diner was here long before I'd even visited South Cove the first time.

Now it was time to add a new member to our family. Evie already had connections with the group. We just needed to make sure she had connections to the community so she'd stay around a while.

I made a quick turkey sandwich for lunch and, after letting out Emma, I was on my way back into town. This time in my Jeep. We'd walk to Main Street Bed and Breakfast, but Bakerstown was just a little too far to do on foot. Especially if I wanted to be back before dark.

I parked in my spot behind the shop and climbed out. Coffee, Books, and More shared the parking with Antiques by Thomas. A large panel van sat on one side of the lot and a motorcycle was parked on the sidewalk under the back balcony. Josh Thomas's Smart car wasn't parked by the electric supply plug. He must be out for the afternoon.

I went in through the back door, making sure to relock it as I entered. I didn't need people coming in the office and getting into things. The worst that could happen was a cheesecake theft, but I didn't want to hurt anyone with the sugar high they'd get.

Deek and Evie were talking. Homer was cuddled in her arms and he saw me before the humans did. He barked and Evie glanced over.

"Are you ready?" I asked her as I retrieved a cheesecake from out of the walk-in and then put a dozen cookies into a box and wrote down a receipt for Aunt Jackie. I always said they were for marketing, but I think she billed me for most of the missing pastries because she knew my sweet tooth. I patted the box. "Deek, I'll be back for this."

Carrying the cheesecake, I moved toward the front door with Evie hurrying after me.

"Why are we taking treats? I thought we were just going to talk to them?" Evie let Homer down on the sidewalk as she caught up with me.

I paused at the corner and looked both ways. No traffic. "Didn't your mama ever tell you it's not nice to go visiting empty-handed?"

"No, but I guess that's true."

I laughed as we crossed the road and headed toward Bill and Mary's bed-and-breakfast. "Neither did mine, but it's a nice sentiment."

We didn't go in the front door when we reached the large, Craftsman-style home. We took a rock path and went around the house and into the backyard. The kitchen door had its own porch, a miniature of the one in the front. Mary's garden was nicely rototilled and there were plants already growing.

"It's lovely back here." Evie stopped to let Homer smell a bush. "That reminds me. The small garden on the back porch—is it okay if I plant some vegetables in pots along with the flowers? I'd love some fresh tomatoes this summer."

"Of course. Aunt Jackie might take some of that furniture, but you can add pots to the mix. There's a fresh-food stand open down by my house if you ever want something else. They bring in a lot of different types of produce at all times of the year." I needed to mention this to Aunt Jackie so it wouldn't shock her. Harrold had set up the first patio garden just for my aunt. He'd done it even though they'd been broken up at that time. He'd told me it might just be the last gift he was able to give her.

"Jill? Are you okay? You seem a little lost." Evie's voice brought me back out of the memory.

I'd hated the thought that my aunt had been on the verge of throwing away her last chance at happiness. I nodded to Homer. "You'd better pick him up; Mary runs a tight kitchen."

When I knocked on the door it was thrown open quickly. Mary Sullivan co-owned the bed-and-breakfast, and my aunt's best friend burst into a huge smile. "Jill, it's so nice to see you. I don't think I've seen you since Jackie's wedding. Come in, and who's your friend?"

"Mary, this is Evie Marshall. She's our new barista and lives in Jackie's old place. She's Sasha's cousin." I stood aside so Evie could come up and into the kitchen.

"So nice to meet you. Jackie's talked a lot about you." Mary leaned down to address Homer. "He's such a cutie."

"Thanks. He's my little man. It's funny how attached you can get to a pet." Evie looked around the large kitchen. "Your house is lovely."

"Thank you. We like it. And we love to share it with others. Which is why the bed-and-breakfast business is so perfect for us." She nodded to the table. "Please sit down. What brings you here?"

"One, I wanted to drop off a cheesecake for you and your guests. I don't think I've been by for a while, so I wanted to leave some bookmarks for the shop and the dessert. Just in case someone needs a referral for a book fix." I handed her the cheesecake. "And two, I'm here for gossip."

"Sounds like we need to pour some coffee, then. Or would you rather have iced tea?"

We got drinks settled, then Mary joined us at the table. She glanced toward the dining room door, which led into the house. "I think the house is empty. Bill just took Steve to Bakerstown to see Doc Ames. He wanted to make arrangements for when the body is released. I think he's planning on leaving on Monday. Unless, of course, Greg asks him to stay."

"How long had they been here?"

"Since Monday. They're frequent visitors. They come for the beach and, of course, to see Esmeralda. They are true believers, if you know what I mean." Mary's voice dropped. She attended the United Methodist Church with Esmeralda but had never questioned her talents. "Well, at least until now. I heard Steve talking to his lawyer on the phone. For some reason he's convinced that Nan's death is all Esmeralda's fault. I didn't interrupt, but boy, I wanted to tell him to think before he judged."

I leaned forward. "Yeah, I heard him say the same thing. Do you know why he would think that?"

Mary sighed and sipped her tea. "The only thing I can think of is that Nan believed Esmeralda could actually talk to their son. Steve, on the other hand, was trying to move on. He wanted to stop the visits here. He told Bill that although he loved the room and the area, he would be glad when they could stop coming here so often."

"How often did they visit?" Evie asked.

Mary pursed her lips, trying to think. "Once a month at least. Of course, the last couple of months it's been every couple of weeks. I guess Nan thought Esmeralda was just about to tell them something about their son. He left the world so troubled. All they wanted to know was that he was fine now. If they'd just had faith, this never would have happened."

"Did he say Esmeralda killed her? Did he see something?"

"Nothing like that. In fact, he didn't even know she was gone that night until Tim arrived the next morning to take him to the station. The poor man burst into tears, right in that chair. He really loved his wife." Mary sighed. "Now he's all alone. Money doesn't buy companionship. Or heal relationships."

"That's for certain." Evie glanced down at Homer. "I need to take him out. I'll meet you outside. Don't hurry on my account."

I watched as Evie ran out of the kitchen. She didn't want to talk about money and relationships, that was clear. I turned back to Mary. "She's a nice woman."

"I wasn't questioning that." Mary looked thoughtfully at the door. "Do you know her story yet? I'm pretty sure if we knew where she was coming from, she might be more understandable for the rest of us."

Chapter 8

Evie and I dropped Homer off at the apartment and picked up the box of cookies before heading into Bakerstown. I wondered if I should follow Mary's advice and see if I could get more information about Evie's past without being intrusive. Or should I just leave it alone, like any normal boss would? The problem was, our team at Coffee, Books, and More wasn't a normal workplace. I knew way too much about most of my employees and I was related to one of them. We were more of a family than just a work team.

I decided to jump in.

"I feel like I don't know a lot about you. Where did you and Homer live before you moved here?" I decided playing dumb might be the best tactic.

"Really? Because I thought I told you I lived in New York just outside the city?" She stared at me through her sunglasses.

I was sure my face was red, but it was hot in the Jeep. I turned up the air. "That's right. You had a big backyard. You were married. I was married once. It didn't take. I think we were just on different paths, you know. He had his career and I had mine. Because we did the same thing—I used to be a lawyer—I guess I thought it would be okay."

"My husband was a politician. I stayed home, but we never had kids." She turned her face away and stared out the window. "Not much of a story there. I married the wrong guy. He liked to use me to deal with the frustrations at work. I could handle myself, but then one night he went after Homer. That wasn't cool. The dog just wanted to greet him."

"I know how I'd react to someone hurting my dog. I was out of town a few months ago for Amy's bridal shower and someone tried to break into my house. If they'd hurt Emma, I would have tried to hurt them before they went to jail." I stared at the sparkling ocean. I'd been freaked out when I'd heard the news from Esmeralda. But she'd stood by Emma and had called the cops when she'd seen the van in my driveway. "Pets need us to protect them. And when I failed I felt horrible."

"You didn't fail. You weren't home." Evie took a tissue out of her purse and dabbed at her cheeks under the sunglasses. "Anyway, once John hurt Homer, we were done. I had to fight to leave, but I wasn't going to back down. He didn't believe me when I told him it was over. I'd taken so much crap over the years, he thought this was too small to cause the breakup."

"You fooled him," I said and let the words settled. The car got quiet for a while. "I didn't mean to pry."

"Oh yes, you did." Evie smiled. "Sasha warned me that you all would be all up in my business and not to take it personally. That you guys just cared too much to let things be. I guess that's why we're doing this, right?"

"This? You mean talking to people about Nan's murder?"

When she nodded I thought about that for a minute. I wasn't sure I had a good answer but decided to try to explain.

"Greg would say I'm too nosy. He worries about me getting into things I can't control. My aunt would say I've got too big of a heart. I'm always trying to fix things for others." I paused for a second. "But I just want the truth to be found. As a lawyer, a lot of times the decisions the courts made weren't about the truth. I don't want someone to die and have the wrong person in jail for it. Or worse, for no one to be brought to justice. It doesn't seem right."

Evie nodded. "I get that. I'm clearly in it for justice. No matter what the cost. Your man seems like he gets it too."

"He does. He just doesn't want me to be the one who gets in front of the killer. He'd prefer that I would be a little more discreet with my investigations. But you don't know things if you don't ask." I turned down the highway and away from the ocean views. "Thanks for telling me. I suspect the breakup must be hard to talk about."

"Not really. It's just that John taught me to be a private person. Mostly to protect him and his crazy view of what family should look like. I need to learn to let more people inside my walls. Maybe being here will be a good thing for me." She pointed to the seaside cottage that held a small tea shop. "That's adorable."

"Well, still, I appreciate getting to know you a bit better. We should do more of these adventures." I parked the car at Bakerstown Funeral Home and turned off the engine.

"Maybe we can go somewhere else next time? Like a park or shopping or something a little less creepy?" Evie looked up at the building.

"This used to be Flannigan's Funeral Home, but Doc Ames changed the name a few years ago when he paid off the loan on the building. He lives in the apartment upstairs. The county morgue is in the basement. And services are held on the main floor. That's where his office is too. So as long as you don't go downstairs or he's not preparing for an event, the chance of running into a dead body is pretty remote. Especially if you stay with me. I'm about as creeped out as you are." I picked up the box of cookies. "You ready?"

"I guess. I could stay out here and wait, but I'd be scared of being alone in the car. A lot of things scare me lately. That's one reason I love the apartment. You did a great job on security for that place." She climbed out of the Jeep and shut the door. "Maybe he's not home?"

"I'll buy you lunch in town after this. To repay your courage." I locked the car and headed to the main door. It was unlocked. Which meant Doc Ames was probably in his office. He shut the main floor down if he was working downstairs or relaxing upstairs. "Looks like we caught him during office hours."

We moved into the velvet-covered foyer. I'd swear there was even more red velvet in the area than the last time I'd been here, but that had to be impossible. Every plush surface, every window was covered with the stuff. The rest of the furniture was polished dark wood. The lights were dim and a scent of floral filled my senses.

"Come this way." I led her to Doc's office and knocked softly.

"Come on in," he called.

I took Evie's arm and opened the door. There the funeral home atmosphere ended. Doc was a pack rat. His desk was filled with files, newspapers, magazines, and books. Lots of books. I moved into the room and set down the cookie box on a file near the middle of his desk. Then I cleaned off the chairs and set the files on the floor. I motioned to Evie to sit.

Doc was focused on his computer. His eyes looked a little bugged out due to his glasses, and his fine, gray hair looked like it hadn't been combed in weeks. He held up a finger as he finished typing with another finger. In a few minutes a smile came over his face and he raised his hands over his head.

"Victory comes to the persistent. At least when you're talking about state forms." He glanced over at us and grinned. "Well now, if I'd known it was two lovely young ladies visiting, I would have let the paperwork sit. Even though it's due today."

"We come bearing gifts." I pointed to the box. "An assortment of Sadie's best. Doc, have you met my new barista, Evie Marshall?"

"Can't say I have. Nice to meet you, Evie. Can I pour you a cup of coffee to go with a cookie?" He pushed his glasses onto the top of his head and smiled at her. The man had the warmest smile on the Central California coast. And that was saying a lot.

"Yes, please, sir," Evie stammered.

"Oh, dear, please don't call me sir. My father was sir. I'm just Doc." He nodded to me. "Coffee for you?"

"Yes, please." I opened the box and took out a cookie with the pile of napkins I'd brought. Vanilla cream. I'd had one when Sadie had dropped them by the first time and I'd fallen in love.

When we'd got settled with coffee and a cookie Doc leaned back in his chair and studied me. "What brings you here, besides introducing your new barista to the oldest man in Bakerstown?"

"That is so not true. I think the guy at the Laundromat has to be older," I teased.

"Harvey is two months younger. We old guys talk." He tapped a pencil on the file under my cookie box. "But you haven't answered my question. Why are you here?"

"Esmeralda's blaming herself for her death and the victim's husband is adding fuel to the fire. He says Esmeralda killed Nan." I set down my coffee. "Is it possible?"

He shrugged. "Who did the deed is outside my line of expertise. But I can tell you that the killer had a lot of upper body strength. I can't discount a woman, but it's unlikely."

I felt my shoulders go down. This was the first good news I'd had all day.

"Of course, our Esmeralda isn't just any woman. She's a bodybuilder. Did you know that? The girl can press two hundred pounds, and that was a year ago, when I saw her compete. Who knows how strong she is now?" He whistled.

"So you can't rule her out." I couldn't hide the disappointment in my voice.

He shook his head. "Sorry. The poor woman was strangled. Then she hit her head on a table in the room. She died instantly on the fall."

"Aren't you a pile of good news today?" I sank back in my chair and ate the cookie. "Anything else you can tell me?"

"If she hadn't died in that painting place, she would have died within the next few weeks anyway. She had advanced, metastasized cancer. She was a walking time bomb. The pain must have been unbearable." He glanced in the cookie box. "I can't believe she wasn't in hospice."

"Mary said they'd been coming more often lately. Maybe she wanted to figure out what was on the other side and that's why they were visiting Esmeralda." Evie turned to me.

"Which explains why she was here. And why she was drinking so heavily on Tuesday night. But who killed her? I can't believe it was Esmeralda. No matter what the reason."

Doc nodded. "I tend to agree with you, but I have no leads for you to work."

"I'm glad to see you anyway. How have you been?"

After about thirty minutes of small talk we were back in the car and heading for the seafood restaurant near the bay. The food there was amazing and I was starving. My mind swirled around Nan and her cancer diagnosis.

"Do you think Steve knew she was dying?" Evie asked as we were getting out of the car.

"That is an interesting question. I don't know. But at least Greg has something to work with there." I pointed to the building. "Have you eaten here yet? The view is lovely and we should be able to sit on the deck today. Unless you want to eat inside."

"You're kidding, right? There's no way you can pry my fingers from the deck chair. It looks totally upscale. Are you sure?" Evie bounced in her seat.

I smiled, glad I'd found a fellow foodie. "Believe me. Let's go eat."

The next hour was spent talking about nothing having to do with murder or work or strained relationships. Evie asked me questions about local people she'd met or heard about and I filled her in on all the dirt in town. It was fun helping someone see South Cove the way I did. On the other hand, I tried to be fair in my stories. Like with Josh Thomas. He had changed so much in the years since I'd known him. He used to dress in an old black suit that I swore he wore every day. With a threadbare white button-down. Then he lost weight. A lot of weight. Gained a girlfriend besides my aunt, and started buying and wearing colors. I'd been so shocked the first time I'd seen him in a polo, I'd almost run into a light pole as I walked by.

I finished my iced tea and glanced at my watch. "I probably need to get home and let Emma out. She's good, but she can only hold it for so long."

"Homer's the same way." Evie smiled. "It took me forever to potty train him, but since we left John, he's been calmer and better about holding it. He's not ruining your apartment or anything, I swear."

"Don't worry about it. I knew you had a pet when you moved in. Life happens." I paid the bill and then stood. "Not to force you to look to the future—and believe me, I don't want a new renter—but are you looking at buying something long-term?"

"I seriously don't know. I like being near family, but the prices out here are crazy. And I come from the New York area. I guess I need to know what I'm going to do with my life too. I love being a barista, especially because I also get to sell books, but it's not a long-term plan. I need a better-paying job. Sasha says I should look at marketing, but I don't want to go back to school."

"Deek's our school expert. I swear, the guy would stay in school for the rest of his life if he could find a way to pay for it. Toby's in the house hunting mode. I think he's going to move out of my shed before the end of the year. He's just saving up for a down payment."

We made our way to the parking lot.

"You have two rentals? Are you looking to expand your real estate holdings?" Evie glanced at me. "I always wondered if I'd like buying and selling real estate. Maybe that's my thing."

"Maybe. I hate being a landlord. And I've only rented to friends and family. It's hard for me to bring up things like missing rent checks. But I haven't had to yet. It's just the fear of the possibility." I started the car and we made our way to the highway and back to South Cove.

"Now, see, I'm the exact opposite. I'm afraid I'd be too aggressive and people would leave me. I tend to say what's on my mind."

"That's a great trait. At least you'll keep it real around the shop. I want you to speak up when you have an idea, and don't let a silly fear stop you."

"The guys are both afraid of your aunt, you know that, right?"

Evie wasn't wrong. I grinned over at her. "We're working on that."

By the time I got Evie back to the apartment and pulled into the driveway at home, it was almost five. I hurried to let Emma outside and checked my mail. Bills, junk, bills, junk, and a wedding invitation from Amy and Justin. The wedding was finally a go. I smiled as I opened the double-enveloped invite and went over to put the date on my calendar. She hadn't given people much notice this time. She'd sent out a save-the-date for the February date, but it had been panned by Justin's family. This time Amy was going ahead with the ceremony no matter what.

I put away the mail in my office, then ran upstairs to change into running clothes. I had time to spare before it got dark, and if I did run, I could justify at least one more cookie when I got back.

I really needed to stop bringing treats home. I said they were for Greg, but to be honest, I think I ate most of them. I clicked on Emma's leash and we were off.

Esmeralda was sitting on her porch when we came back and I crossed the road with Emma to go talk to her.

"Go away. I'm in a bad mood." She sipped from her wineglass. I noticed she'd brought out the bottle with her.

"I'm just checking on my friend. Have you rethought quitting? Greg needs you." I sat next to her on the swing, and Emma nuzzled her hand until she started petting her.

"I don't want him to be compromised by this situation." Esmeralda rubbed Emma behind her ears.

"I'm sorry, maybe I'm misunderstanding. Did you kill Nan?" I didn't focus on her, just sat.

She waited a heartbeat, then sighed. "Of course not. I'm a pacifist. I don't even like eating meat. It clogs the senses, and my spirit contact says it makes me smell."

"Then why would working at the station compromise Greg at all? The woman was sick. She was dying. Maybe someone wanted to help her out of her pain?" I hadn't meant to let Doc's message to me be broadcast to everyone, but Esmeralda needed to know.

Her hand stilled and she lifted it from Emma's back to lay still on the edge of the swing. She glanced at me, then spoke. "I know that. I'm the one who told her she was dying."

Chapter 9

When Greg finally got home that night I was on the couch watching an old movie. I had a pint of ice cream in hand. He came in, sat next to me, and took the spoon and carton away from me and started eating. I leaned my head on his shoulder. "Have my bad eating habits worn off on you?" He kissed the top of my head. "I'm just trying to save you from yourself. This is a sacrificial act."

"That tastes amazing." I turned down the sound. "I need to talk to you."

"You and every other person in South Cove. Half the people are in the pro-Esmeralda camp. The other half think this is a fine time to reinstitute the practice of burning witches." He finished the last bite of ice cream. "Any more of this in the freezer? I didn't eat much dinner."

"No, but there are leftover chicken wings from Monday in the fridge." There really was more ice cream, but I was being the good girlfriend and aiming him toward something a little healthier. At least that was my story.

"Can you put them in the microwave for me? And grab me a beer? I don't think I can make it to the kitchen." He kicked off his shoes and flexed his toes. "I've never been this tired."

"You're worried about Esmeralda." I stood and headed to the kitchen. It was time to let Emma out anyway. And I needed a soda. "Hold that thought. I'll be right back."

Emma went out first. Then I put the wings in the microwave and got our drinks. Taking them back into the living room, I sat for a minute. "Look, I talked to Esmeralda. She feels guilty because her spirit guide told Nan she was dying. That she needed to go to the doctor."

"And now she's dead. You're not helping her case here." He closed his eyes. "Sorry if that came out grumpy."

"No worries. But you didn't let me finish. Instead of going to the doctor, Nan started seeing more psychics. She wanted to know if she was going to join her son. Esmeralda kept trying to tell her to go to the doctor, but she ignored her. Finally, on this trip, Esmeralda told Nan if she wasn't going to go to the doctor, she was going to tell Steve, and not see her in sessions any more. Well, I guess that caused a fight and Esmeralda showed her the door. That was Tuesday morning." I held up a finger when I heard Emma barking. "Hold a second."

When I came back with a plate of wings and napkins and Emma on my heels, Greg was scribbling on his notepad. He tossed the pen and book on the coffee table and took the plate. "Esmeralda feels guilty because the woman died and she could have stopped her, except that she was murdered and didn't just die of natural causes."

"Doc says she would have died a few weeks later. Any chance she could have died of natural causes anyway?" I asked Greg the same question I'd asked Doc, just in case there might be a different answer.

"She just happened to have someone's hands around her neck?" Greg shook his head and wiped the barbecue sauce from his chin. "Not a chance."

"But if Esmeralda didn't kill her, who did?" I crossed my legs under me and thought about the question. "What about Steve? It's usually the husband, right? There's a book about that."

"There probably is. Anyway, I appreciate your information, but no, we're not sharing theories here. Did you find out anything else?" He finished the last of the wings and stood, waiting for her answer.

"Not much, just that they were coming here a lot the last few months." I stood and followed him into the kitchen. "And you know what Doc told me. The good thing about my day was the time I got to spend with Evie. She's funny and easy to talk to."

"I would expect no less from Sasha's cousin." He rinsed his plate and put it into the dishwasher, along with my ice cream spoon. "I'm crashing. I'll probably leave before you get up, so give me two kisses. One for tonight and one for the morning."

"You're a dork." But I kissed him anyway.

"I'm not a dork." He tapped my nose afterward. "Face it, I'm a hopeless romantic."

* * * *

The next morning, true to his word, Greg was already gone when I woke. I got ready for work and wondered what my volume would be today. It made me a little sad that everyone in town didn't support Esmeralda, but I guess I could understand those who thought she was a little off. But there were more things we didn't understand than we did.

Darla sat at one of my tables outside the shop. "You're late."

"You're early. Seriously, you've got to stop stalking me. People will start to talk." I unlocked the door and we went inside. I started my morning routine, then made us both coffees. "I found out a little yesterday."

"Tell me, because I got nothing. The guys were both out canvassing the town. And by the time they got back, Greg was already back at the station. He runs a tight ship over there, even without Esmeralda to be his guard dog."

I relayed everything I'd found out about the murder to Darla, which really wasn't much, but she seemed happy with the update. We agreed to meet tomorrow and update each other on anything we found out. Just before she left, she glanced at the back door into the office. "How did your time with Evie go? Is she going to fit in at South Cove?"

"I think so. She's interesting and funny and likes food almost as much as I do." I grinned, knowing that Darla had a love affair with food as well. "Why do you ask?"

She shrugged, uncomfortable. "I don't know. People are just rude sometimes. If you like her, I'm sure I will as well."

"You painted with her; what did you think?"

"About the same. I'm just hearing some grumbling at the winery. You know every newcomer has to run the gauntlet here in South Cove. I'm sure she'll find her place soon." Darla paused, then pointed a finger at me. "I know. Maybe she should come to the Young Female Professional Club next Wednesday night. We meet at the winery and talk about our lives and how the glass ceiling is holding us down."

"You own your winery. Nobody is holding you down," I pointed out the obvious.

Darla laughed. "You'd be surprised at all the crap I get from men who don't know I'm the owner. Last week a new supplier wouldn't talk to me, wanted to meet with Matt, the owner. He introduced them to me, then left to fix a sink in the men's bathroom. I'm thinking I'm not going to carry their wine just because they're jerks."

"Go get them." I watched her leave and thought about the times salesmen had come in the shop and asked to talk to the owner. And when I introduced myself, I got comments about how young and pretty I was to be running such a large business. They'd made me want to punch them. But instead I voted with my checkbook. I never bought from those salesmen if I could help it. Maybe joining a social group would help Evie fit in better, but I wasn't sure the girl power club was exactly her jam. Evie was already confident and in charge of her life. At least she was now.

I chose a book and went to the couch to read. Apparently, no one needed coffee today because there had been no updates or possible killer theories handed out to the public. A woman in a black business suit came in about thirty minutes later. I'd already served most of my commuters, but maybe this woman was new to the area. "Good morning. Are you here for coffee or some reading material?"

"Coffee, please. Large black with just a splash of sugar-free hazelnut, please. Although now that I think about it, I'll grab a couple of books while I'm here. I came out here in a rush and didn't pack any reading material. I almost died from boredom last night, watching what passes for television shows nowadays. Talk about preaching to the lowest common denominator."

"What do you like to read? Maybe I can make some suggestions." I poured the coffee and handed it to her after adding a few shots of flavor.

"Don't worry about it. I have specific tastes. Your bookstore is so quaint, I hope you have a least a few of the current best sellers." She took the cup and sipped. "This is perfect. Okay if I pay with my book purchase? That way I don't have to track all the different receipts."

"Not a problem." I nodded to the couch. "I'll be over there reading if you have any questions."

A few minutes into her book search her phone rang. She picked it up and held it with her shoulder. "Candice Frey, may I help you?"

I tried to tune out the discussion, right up to the point when Candice asked the caller, "What if this were you in the situation? You would be out of your head crazy with grief. I'm surprised that Steve's even talking. If it's not an emergency, let's just lean back a minute and give him time to grieve. I'll deal with anything the company needs on my end."

I wrote down her name on the notepad I kept near me just in case something jogged my memory as I read. Either Candice was a family friend or Steve's lawyer. Or both. I'd research her after she left my shop. As I watched, she went over to the romances, quickly picked out three of the new paranormal releases, and then went to nonfiction business self-help stuff. Deek had been increasing the number of titles we carried, and because of his curation, we'd sold more nonfiction since he'd joined the team.

Which reminded me: I needed to talk to Evie about what genre she liked to read and what section of ARCs she wanted to be responsible for.

I wrote another note on my pad. Then I watched as Candice carried six books to the register. My aunt was always over the moon when I sold two books over a shift. Today she'd be ecstatic.

"Are you good, then?" I picked up one of the paranormal romances. "I think we have the complete trilogy here for this author if you get done before you leave town. I can set them aside for you."

Candice nodded her head. "Go ahead and grab them for me. I'd rather have too much to read than not enough."

I ran over to the shelf and picked out the other two books. Deek had also set up a purchasing system so our weekly buy list reordered the books we'd sold the week before. That way, we always had the most recent best seller on hand. If it was older, sometimes we had to special order, but not recently.

I rang up each book and glanced at the two hardbacks. The first was about getting over grief and the other one was titled *Getting a Date— Lessons for the Urban Professional.*

I scanned the bar code, then opened the book to the title page. It was signed by the author. "Temperance came to the shop right after her first book tour and did a signing. I don't have anyone scheduled this week, but if you're in town for a couple of weeks, I have a debut woman's fiction author talking next Thursday."

"I hope I won't be here, but thanks for the invite." She held open the book and grinned. "I don't think I've ever had a real autographed book before. Typically, I order online. Not digital, though, I don't want to spend any more time on my computer than I need to."

"I love print books too." I bagged the books and gave her the total. She didn't blink but handed me a credit card. "What brings you to South Cove? Vacation?"

The woman shook her head. "No, someone I knew had the unfortunate pleasure of being killed here. I'm here to help her husband get out of town without being arrested for murder or doing something stupid."

* * * *

Deek came in a few minutes later with his laptop to write a few hours. I think he liked the easy access to coffee and treats. He set up his area, then came over to pour a cup.

"Hey, boss, how's the day going?" He leaned on his arms, watching me. Or probably watching my aura.

"It's been interesting. A few customers. I sold that fantasy trilogy for the new author and the last signed dating book."

"I told you people would eat up those books. She's going to be famous. Just wait." He leaned his head over and studied me. "You're pretty calm for a murder investigation going on."

"Not my monkeys, not my circus." I eyed the cup supply. Maybe I should refill now instead of waiting until the shift was nearly over.

"And another discrepancy. It's always your business when one of these things happens. Why is this different?" He sipped his coffee and watched for my response.

"Maybe I'm just taking another path. The road-less-traveled kind of thing?" I started a list of supplies I needed for the back.

"I think you protest too much, but I've got words to get done before my shift and I have a date after work. So it's now or never."

"Good writing." I sounded like some crazed motivational coach. I went back to my reading and ignored the cups that needed refilling.

Near the end of my shift my cell rang just as I finished the chores. Aunt Jackie had set up for each shift ending and beginning. She was a firm believer that systems worked in running a business. I think she must have read it in some business book and simplified it for our situation. I checked the caller ID, then answered Amy's call with a smile. "Hey, don't tell me you're free for lunch. Or are you standing me up for brunch?"

Sundays were our standard brunch days. Just the two of us. We'd done it for years and having at least a weekly connection had kept our friendship strong. Strong enough that Amy's crazy bridezilla act of the last year hadn't made me run screaming.

"What? Lunch today, no, sorry. Look, I'm trying to find Justin. I haven't seen him since Wednesday and we were supposed to go finalize the catering today, but he's not at his apartment. His mail is just scattered all over the floor. Do you think he ran?" Amy's questions got faster and faster as she asked, but the last one made her stop talking. I could hear the sharp intake of breath as she considered the answer.

"No. He didn't run. Maybe he just went to take care of something and forgot about the caterer. Can you postpone it or does it have to be done today?"

"It can't be postponed. If we're having this wedding at the end of the month, we have to finalize today. I don't want to just choose for him, especially in the state I'm in." She laughed harshly. "Yes, I know I'm being impossible. I could be so bad I'd cause the caterer to fire me as a client. Then what would I do?"

"What time is the tasting and where?" I glanced at my watch. If I left now, I could get to Bakerstown in thirty minutes. But any later and I'd run into traffic that slowed to watch the ocean.

"Twelve thirty. I've only got twenty minutes to find him and get to the caterers. They're over by the supermarket in that same building. Why?" I could hear the panic in Amy's voice.

"Because I'm coming to help you finalize the catering. If I'm right, Justin will meet you there and I'll just go do my shopping for the week. I have to come into town anyway. And if he doesn't show, we can get this done, then go sit at a bar and talk about where he might be and what a jerk he was for not coming." I glanced at the table where Deek had been writing, but he was already packed up and walking to the counter. I covered the mouthpiece, but he waved me away.

"Go save Amy. I was stuck at a spot anyway. Sometimes I don't know if I wrote something or not, so I have to go back and check the last few scenes. Writing is a lot of hard work." He tucked his tote under the counter and slipped on an apron, starting his shift opening list of to-dos.

"Thanks." I went back to the phone. "Okay, Amy, I'll meet you at the caterers. Call me if you run into Justin before I get there."

"I'm heading there now." Amy paused, then said, "Thanks, Jill. You're the best."

"Don't I know it." I tucked my phone into my tote and headed home. Today was one of those days I wished I'd driven to work, but no luck. Josh stood at his door and tried to wave me down. "Sorry, Josh, I have an emergency."

"We can talk later," he called after me. "I hope Greg's all right."

I hadn't said it was Greg, but if I didn't correct him, by the time I'd gotten back from Bakerstown, rumors would be flying of Greg's accident. "It's Amy. She has a wedding emergency."

"Oh." Now Josh looked green. "Go, fix her. Brides-to-be are scary."

As I hurried home, I wondered if Josh and Amy had had an encounter in the last few weeks. I'd have to get the story from Amy. Josh didn't know a lot about women, so he was scared of most of them. Except me. Me, he hated, and pushed me to do what he thought was my job as coordinator for the business community. I just had different ideas that he didn't like.

Josh didn't flinch from talking to me. How did I get so lucky?

I let Emma out for a quick run around the yard as I changed into a nicer pair of jeans and a spring-colored tank. I slipped on my flower flip-flops and ran some goop through my hair to make it bounce. Good enough.

I made it to Bakerstown Catering in twenty-nine minutes. Just don't ask me what the legal speed limit is for Highway 1.

As I pulled up to the front, I saw Amy sitting on a bench outside the front doors, crying.

I took a deep breath. If Justin had broken things off, I was going to kill him the next time I saw him. And there would be no way Greg would finger me for the deed. Justin would just disappear.

I hurried to my friend, hoping I wouldn't have to make good on my oath because I had no way to really kill someone. Especially because I hated the sight of blood and had no upper arm strength. "Amy, what's wrong?"

"He texted me. He said he was sorry, but he couldn't change his plans." Amy sobbed and pointed to the catering door. "Sorry? This is our wedding and he's too busy to help?"

"Maybe it's work. You know he's close to being tenured." I pulled her into a hug. "Let's just get this done; then we can go drink at that little bar and grill you like on Highway 1. I'll buy."

"You think he's just busy with work?" Amy tried to take a deep breath, but it caught in her throat three times before she could get in control of the sobs. "That would make sense. I know he was trying to wrap up as much as possible for the end of the semester before we left on the honeymoon."

"Justin loves you," I reminded her. "Sometimes men make the wrong choices."

She took a compact from her purse and laughed at her image. "Racoon eyes. I'm going to have to redo all my makeup before we do pictures."

"Of course," I said. But my head had already gone to a new place. We were taking pictures of the tasting? My friend was documenting every step of the way to the final wedding. No wonder Justin chose work over this.

Chapter 10

After eating bits and bites of everything that would be on the menu, I wasn't starving, but I was still hungry. When we got to the bar the first thing I did was get menus. Greg wouldn't be home, so this could be lunch and dinner. By the time I got home the food would have settled enough that I could take Emma for a run.

This was turning out to be a pretty great day. Or it would be if I didn't have a worried bride on my hands.

Amy glanced over the menu, then ordered her usual small meal: a double cheeseburger, fries, and a chocolate shake. I went totally off the wall and ordered a scallop basket with fries and a cup of New England clam chowder. And a vanilla shake. Maybe I'd give it another hour before I ran with Emma.

"Do you want a beer or a drink?" I handed her the cocktail menu. "I'm designated driver, so if you wanted something, go ahead."

She shook her head. "I don't want to leave my car in town. I'd rather have it at the apartment with me. I have a beer or two at the house. If I want a drink, I'll have one there."

"Justin's fine. He's just busy. You get that, right?" I studied my friend as she set aside the cocktail menu.

"I do. The wedding is just so close. I like him to at least touch base with me so I feel like we're doing this together." She studied me. "I'm not making a mistake here, am I? I mean, you and Greg are great together, but you two aren't planning a huge party to tell the world that you're a couple."

"Someday we will, and you can be the one to have this conversation with me. Look, you both want this wedding. You both have made these plans. He's just trying to clear his desk so he can be focused on the wedding prep for the last two weeks." At least that was what I hoped he was doing. He'd told me he'd stop in to chat about his possible honeymoon choices, yet I hadn't seen him at the shop. He needed to get reservations made before they'd be renting a room at one of the local no-tell motels on the highway. But I wasn't telling Amy that. She'd go through the roof.

"How do you always make me feel better?" Amy pulled out her notebook. "I'm updating my chart really quickly to see what else I can get done while I'm in Bakerstown. Do you want to visit the venue with me after we eat? I need to check on the entry to the ballroom."

"I probably need to get home to let Emma out. She's been pretty antsy lately. And I think I forgot to put up the sofa pillows before I left." I had just totally lied to my best friend. Emma had been wonderful for almost six months and I had put away the sofa pillows, but I didn't want to go measure a ballroom and poke holes in the idea of having the wedding there. Sooner or later Amy was going to have to lock the wedding ideas in the safe and just have a good day.

Amy excused herself to go to the restroom, and while she was gone, the food arrived. The milkshake wasn't quite as good as the ones from Diamond Lille's, but the scallop basket and the chowder were actually better. But don't tell Tiny I said that. Lille's chef, Tiny, took the food he prepared personally.

When she came back she was chuckling.

"What's got you happy again?" I glanced around the room, not seeing anything I would find funny.

"Just people watching. There's a couple over in the last booth by the bathrooms. They're totally inappropriate for each other. He's older, so I'm thinking it's a clandestine affair. Maybe they live in the city and drove out here for some privacy?" Her face froze. "Oh, no..."

"What now?"

"What if Justin just needed one last fling?"

"Amy, Justin loves you. He's crazy about you. And if he says he's working, well, you need to take him at his word." I waited for her to calm her breathing. "Just because some people cheat doesn't mean all marriages end that way. Besides, you don't know that they aren't married to each other and this is just some sort of foreplay with them."

I glanced over to the booth Amy had pointed out and froze. "Well, I'll be..."

Amy sensed the change of tone in my words before I said anything more. "You recognize them."

It was a statement, not a question. Without thinking, I answered. "The guy is Steve Gunter and that's Candice Frey, his lawyer."

"Who appears to be very close to the grieving husband," Amy observed. "You're right. This totally has gotten my mind off my missing fiancé. Now I want to know if Greg's going to arrest the husband, the mistress, or both?" I pulled out my phone. "Let's just drop a bee in the bouquet and get things moving here. I know Greg hadn't talked with Steve yet because the man had been too grief-stricken to talk about his wife."

Amy held out her hand. "Wait, this is just like the couple that was supposed to be managing our charity run a few years ago. He'd been cheating on the dead wife, right?"

"Yeah." I stared at the couple in the booth. "This sure looks like the same thing. Maybe Greg can find out what's going on."

"Or we could just go over and ask why he's not torn up about his poor wife?" Amy's eyes were bright. I could see she totally wanted to confront the couple.

"Greg wouldn't like it. And what happens if we do and they disappear to some island without extradition laws? Esmeralda would still be suspect number one." I dialed Greg's number and, when he actually answered, explained the situation to him.

"And you're telling me you just happened to be there? You and Amy didn't follow Steve to this meeting?" Greg's tone was dry.

"I'm almost offended except I would have totally done something like that. Anyway, no, it was just bad luck we showed up here. Do you want us to go find out what's going on with the two of them?"

"No. I do not. It just so happens I'm in Bakerstown, and I'll be there in a few minutes. Just eat your lunch and ignore them."

I glanced over at the table that was filled with beer bottles and not much food. "What if they try to leave?"

"Let them. Jill, you're a civilian in another jurisdiction. If you get in trouble here, I might not be able to get you out." He sighed when I didn't answer. "Look, I'm almost there. Just stay put."

I hung up the phone and put it in my purse.

Amy leaned closer and whispered, "Are we supposed to go over to interrogate them?"

"No. We're supposed to eat our lunch and let the trained professionals do their job. But I have an idea." I called over our waitress. "See the couple in the booth over there? Would you hold on to their check if they try to cash out? That's my husband's best friend and they haven't seen each other in a long time. He'll be here in just a few minutes."

The girl smiled. "I can do that. Although I don't think they'll be leaving soon; they just ordered food."

"Perfect. Thanks for your help." I turned back to Amy. "There we go."

"She'll know you lied when the police show up."

"Not my usual restaurant. And I'll leave a good tip." I focused on finishing my lunch.

When Greg came in he stopped by our booth first. "Where are they?" I nodded toward the booth. "Over there."

"Who's the girl?" He slipped onto the bench next to me and ate a few of my fries.

"That's Candice Frey. She came into the shop this morning and got some books to read because she's going to be stuck here. Then I heard her talking about Steve to someone at his company." I filled him in on what I knew.

"Okay, then. See you at home." He glanced at the food. "Are you two about done?"

"We can be," Amy said. "But I'd really like to stay to see the show."

"Jill can call you once I fill her in tonight. Let's just get you guys out of here and on your way home, okay?" He stared at both of us.

"Yes, Greg." I waved our waitress over. "I'm going to the store before I head home."

He pulled out his wallet. "My treat for the information. CIs get paid."

"And snitches get stitches," Amy added. "Let's get out of here."

Amy had followed me in her car from the catering place, so I told her goodbye and headed back to the supermarket to do my shopping. I'd add a couple of quarts of ice cream, just in case it took Greg some time to get home tonight.

When I got to the market I saw Justin coming out of the catering place. I parked nearby, then climbed out of my car. "You're a little late."

He blushed and turned my way, slipping on his sunglasses as he walked over to me. "Yeah, that's what they said. But they showed me the food you guys picked. The reception is going to be amazing."

"So why didn't you just come to the tasting?" I decided to push. "Amy's freaking out. She thinks—well, she thinks all kinds of things."

He kicked at the cement curb that separated the parking lot from the sidewalk. "I'm trying to avoid her."

My stomach turned just a little bit. "What? You don't want to get married? What are you thinking?"

He held up his hands. "I didn't say I didn't want to get married, but I have a lead on this really cool honeymoon spot I can't check out until tomorrow, so I can't see her until I've got it booked. You know how bad I am at keeping secrets. Maybe I shouldn't see her until the ceremony?"

I shook my head in disbelief. "Are you kidding me? She already thinks the wedding's off. Can't you just call her or something?"

He patted his phone. "I'll call her and tell her I had to fly back to Nebraska because my mom fell. She'd believe that. Mom's not too sturdy on her feet. But you can't tell her you saw me. Otherwise she's going to know somethings up."

"You want me to lie to my best friend and keep your secret just because you can't?" I leaned on my car, letting my words sink in.

"Yes, perfect. I knew you'd understand." He gave me a quick hug, then started to leave down the sidewalk.

"Justin, if you're lying to me, I'm going to track you down and feed you to the fishes."

He paused and spun around to watch me. "Well, isn't that idea kind of cliché?"

"Okay, I'll ask Deek to make up a murder method and then I'll kill you using his instructions. He probably needs the extra credit in his fiction writing class anyway." I didn't move from my spot leaning on the Jeep.

"Seriously, Justin, you'd better not hurt my friend."

"Hurting Amy is the last thing I want to do." He smiled, waved, then took off at a trot down the sidewalk to his car.

I watched him go, then nabbed a cart from the parking area. No one returned carts in this lot and I thought maybe having too many different businesses surrounding it was probably why. No one worried about common courtesy any more. Especially not people I considered my friends.

I tucked my rant into my mental pocket and went inside the grocery store. Time to refill the cupboards.

When I got home Emma waited for me by the door. She took one sniff of the bag I carried, then ran to the kitchen door. She needed out. I left her in the back as I carried in the groceries, which kept me from worrying about her getting out the front. She hadn't so far, but that didn't mean she didn't know how. I think my dog knew a lot of things she wasn't admitting to when you got down to it.

I considered leaving out one of the ice cream containers, but one look at Emma's brown eyes convinced me otherwise. She'd been very good while I got things done. And bonus, she hadn't even tried to eat the couch pillows for the last two days while I'd left her alone for the afternoon. I needed to take her running to burn off any excess energy she still had built up. "Let me get changed."

I got a bounce and a single woof in reply as she went to sit by the back door. She knew exactly what I'd said. Experts say dogs understand about two hundred and fifty human words. I don't know if their brain shuts down after learning those or if they just get bored with us talking so much, but Emma knew a lot.

Once we got on the beach I was surprised to see it almost empty. It was a lovely afternoon and there were fewer than twenty people doing random activities like jogging or playing in the chilly water. Or just sitting on a blanket reading. That was my favorite beach activity. At least once Emma was worn down from the run. Today I'd considered bringing a book but decided my couch would be much more comfortable while I read. Besides, I didn't know when Greg was getting home.

The ice cream sitting in my freezer had nothing to do with the decision. Really.

The run was glorious, and by the time I'd turned around my heart was beating out of my chest. And then I saw Toby standing on the steps to the parking area. Emma barked like she'd seen her friend too. Emma had no human enemies, at least none that hadn't tried to break into her house.

I slowed my pace and got my breath under control. I'd run intervals for the rest of the time. I'd just finished my third speed round when Toby moved from his spot on the stairs and headed out to meet me.

"What are you doing here?" He gave me a short hug and leaned down to do the same to Emma. I think he would have hugged her first except I was one of his bosses. I was also his landlord, his other boss's girlfriend, and a friend. Lines were hard to keep straight in South Cove. I was amazed there weren't more people related to others.

"Running to starve off the ice cream I know I'll eat later." I wiped my face with a handkerchief. Well, it was really a paper towel I'd stuck in my pocket. "What are you doing here?"

"Rumor has it that you got a letter from Sasha. What did she say? Are they happy there?" He glanced at the ocean while he ran through the questions on his list. Of course he didn't ask the big one: was she still in love with Toby or had she moved on? "What did she say?"

"She said she's fine. And so is Olivia. Can you believe she's almost six?" I nodded to the stairs that rose to the parking lot. "Look, I need to talk to you, but if you're all brokenhearted still we can wait."

"That's sensitive of you." He slugged my arm. "I was never 'all brokenhearted.' I was just under the impression that Sasha and I were building a future together. I was wrong."

"You're saying that you're over her?" I wasn't sure if Toby was just lying to me or he was actually lying to himself.

"Totally. Except for just a bit of my heart that's singed, that's all." He paused as we finished the steps. "Tell me what's going on with Olivia. I care for the girl, even if she's not going to be my future daughter."

"She's turning six and they're having a party for her in the city. We're invited, but Greg and I aren't going. I'm sending a gift with Evie. Sasha said she'd leave it to me to tell you. Or not." I studied his face. "I know her leaving hit you hard."

"Jill, it's okay. I'm a big boy. Sasha never said she was going to stay with me forever. She never made promises or vows. But there's something you're not telling me. Why wouldn't you tell me?" He cocked his head and studied me. "Oh, I get it. Sasha's dating someone and he'll be at the party. Maybe I *should* go."

"Toby," I started to warn him about going off on a guy just because he was dating Sasha, but he held up his hand.

"I was kidding. Can you tell Evie I'd like her to take up my gift too? I'll bring it to the shop next week and help her load it. She drives an SUV, right?" He paused at the side of the road and looked both ways. Emma turned her head and followed his directions. Sometimes my dog is more human than some people I know.

"Why? How big is your gift?" We crossed the road and started walking up the hill.

He ignored my question and pointed to Esmeralda's house. "Isn't that Steve Gunter trying to break into Esmeralda's? The guy never learns. Stay here and call it in."

He sprinted across the road as I pulled out my phone. Toby won. He had Steve on the ground, his hand behind his back before I could even dial Greg's number.

Greg answered on the first ring. "What's going on? Where are you?"

"Outside watching Toby hold down Steve Gunter. He was trying to break into Esmeralda's house." I explained the situation.

Greg sighed. "Bring Emma into the yard and tell Toby I'm bringing over the handcuffs."

Chapter 11

Greg stopped back at the house before going into the station. He went to the kitchen, chose a soda, and then dropped on the couch next to me, where I was trying to work on a book review for the newsletter. In truth, I'd mostly been watching the excitement through my front window. Tim had already loaded Steve up in the police cruiser and had left a few minutes ago. I'd watched Toby and Greg talking to Esmeralda for a while on the porch.

"What a mess." He sank into the couch and opened the can.

I waited for him to finish drinking before I asked the question that had been worrying me. "How's Esmeralda?"

"Scared, but she won't show it. I've worked with her long enough that I can see it in her body language. I'm just happy she keeps the front door locked now. If he'd been able to get inside, I'm not sure she'd be okay. He was ranting again about how it was all her fault. Then, when Toby had him cuffed, the guy broke down in tears. He's a mess. When I left him in Bakerstown I thought he was going to head back to the bed-and-breakfast to get some sleep."

"He really blames her for his wife's death? What about the girl he was having drinks with? Maybe she killed his wife to get her out of the way of their happily ever after?" I didn't have much sympathy for a guy who was that callous with his marriage.

"Jill, there's something you need to know…." Greg's phone beeped and he glanced at the display. "That was quick. I need to get to the station. Steve's lawyer's already there."

"Of course she is." I turned back to my laptop where I stared at the three lines I'd actually written in the last hour. "Home late?"

"Home late." He kissed me and gave Emma's head a rub. "Keep an eye on our Jill, okay, girl?"

"I don't need a protector," I called after him.

He paused at the door and grinned. "I think of Emma more as a therapy dog. Maybe she can keep you out of trouble."

"Go to work." I looked around and considered throwing a sofa pillow at him, but Emma would take that as an invitation to play and chew on the thing, and I kind of liked the new ones I'd bought last month, after the last unfortunate incident.

"Love you too." Greg locked the door, then pulled it shut. That was the one thing about living with someone from law enforcement: You found out about the dark side of the world real fast. Even though he didn't like talking about his work and the people he arrested, he did things like lock our front door when we left. And the last time I'd left my laptop in my car in the driveway, I'd gotten a lecture about making it easy to steal from me.

I knew he meant well, but sometimes I wanted to think the world was filled with positive energy and good vibes, not crime and hate.

What can I say, it was my sunshine filter on the world and I was happy with it. I'd worked in family law. I knew there was evil out there. I just didn't want to acknowledge it in my life.

True to his word, Greg didn't come home that night. Well, not until after I'd fallen asleep. Mid morning, my phone rang and a smile crossed my lips as I looked at the caller ID. Amy would brighten my mood with all her wedding talk. "Hey, Amy, what's going on in the tule-filled world of wedding planning?"

"Jill, something's terribly wrong. I went to Justin's office to talk to him about the catering decisions we'd made and they said he took a week of vacation. He told me he was working. What am I going to do?"

"Where are you?"

"Just coming back from Bakerstown. I'm about to turn off the highway." She sniffed. "I've been trying to think all the way back, but I keep coming back to the undeniable fact that he's left me."

"Justin hasn't left you. I talked to him yesterday when I went shopping after our lunch. He said he had to run back to Nebraska to check on his mom." I squeezed my eyes shut. I wasn't supposed to say that. "Look, stop at the house. We'll drink a few beers and figure out this thing with Justin."

"I'm dropping off the car at the apartment. Then I'll walk back. Give me twenty minutes." She paused a beat and I could hear the turn signal in her car. "Thanks Jill, you're the best."

After I hung up I looked at Emma. "Your aunt Amy's coming over for a visit and we need to be very nice to her right now because she's fragile." Emma put her paw on my hand, and I imagined her thinking, *we're a team, Jill. No problem.*

Instead, she was probably asking for a piece of the cheesecake her nose had told her was hanging out in my purse. But, of course, there wasn't any cheesecake in my purse. I'd eaten my piece at the store before I'd left. I hurried and finished my review and sent it off to Deek. I'm sure I was the last one to return their review, even though we'd all had the same deadline. I liked to push boundaries.

I'd just closed the laptop when Amy knocked on the door. I let her in and she set down several boxes on the coffee table. "I thought we could fold napkins into rings while we talked."

"Napkin rings?" Who thought of this kind of stuff? There were other things I'd wanted to say but bit my tongue. The adults who were attending Amy's party knew how to find a napkin and put it on their lap. Well, except for her uncle Brent, who was playing his part well as wedding financier; I was pretty sure he was making notes on everything he paid for.

"Relax, I'm not asking you to paint the Mona Lisa."

"Funny girl." I picked up several books I'd had strung along the couch and carried them to my office. I stacked them on the desk right next to last month's advanced readers copy pile. I wondered how many pounds of books the desk would actually hold. This was getting out of hand. "Can you give me a minute?"

"Sure. I'll set up." Amy disappeared into the kitchen.

I ran upstairs to change out of my running clothes and into sweats. I hadn't done it when I first came home, worried that I would miss seeing something over at Esmeralda's. The poor woman must have been scared in that house with a crazy guy pounding on the door. What was he thinking?

My concern about the scene next door disappeared when I got back to the kitchen. Gray napkins and pearl rings were stacked neatly in two piles, one on each side of the table. Apparently Amy hadn't been joking about me participating in the napkin folding ritual. At least she would until she saw my first fold job. Then I'd be relegated to some paper-pushing task instead. My friend was nothing if not predictable.

She leaned on the table, staring at the piles. "Just tell me there's going to be a wedding. Justin loves me, right?"

"Yes, Justin loves you. There's going to be a wedding. This is just a hiccup. You know how his family is. I'm sure he'll be in touch as soon as he can." I paused by her side. "Do you need to hug it out or something?"

"You're kidding, right? I'm not that kind of girl." She wiped the tears from her cheeks and pasted a fake grin on her face. "Let's get crafting. Tell me about the investigation. What did Greg find out about the grieving husband and his side piece?"

I stepped around to my side of the table and poured myself a cup of coffee. Amy glared at me and I took a sip, then set it back on the counter. "I'll drink over here, away from the totally washable napkins."

"You mean dry-cleanable, don't you?" Amy folded the first one, checking the way it looked in the ring. "Anyway, what's going on with the couple at the restaurant?"

"Actually Greg didn't say much. We had a few other things going on." Everything had been moving so fast, I only knew it was Saturday because I didn't have to work tomorrow, which made that Sunday.

"That's odd. Or was he just bone-tired when he got home?"

I thought about the discussion. "He started to say something when he had to go corral Steve for trying to break down Esmeralda's door."

"OMG. Why didn't you tell me this first? Is Greg all right? Is she?" Amy stared at me, the folded napkin fanning out as she let it set on the table.

"You were in a bit of a panic." I sat down at the table and scooted my chair away from the napkins. "Sit down now and I'll walk you through yesterday's fun show."

I went through everything, including a bit about talking to Toby. I didn't tell the entire story there because betraying his confidence wasn't on my agenda.

Amy eyed me as I finished. "You know Toby's still hung up on Sasha, right? The bride who wasn't a bride from Greg's friend's bachelor party called him and he blew her off."

Now that I hadn't known. I knew Jessica had been interested in Toby, but she was still technically in the grieving process. Or she should be since she lost her fiancé recently. "You mean Jessica? When did that happen?"

Amy shrugged. "A few weeks ago. He and Justin were out for a drink after work one Friday night and she called him. Toby blew it off like it wasn't a big thing, but you know how bad he had it for Sasha. He was seeing white picket fences and everything."

If I'd known about Jessica's call, I wouldn't have been so delicate about Sasha and her new guy. "Toby needs to start dating again. He's a great catch. Someone's out there waiting to be the right one."

"Some hearts take longer to heal than others." Amy glanced at the pile of napkins. "If I could do this whole thing over, Justin and I would have just eloped and sent out announcements. Do you know how much money we would have saved?"

"A lot." I didn't want to encourage her to talk about the wedding. "Look, this is going to be a special day for you and Justin. And if I complain about folding napkins again, just slap me."

"I can't. I'm much stronger than you are. I'll break your jaw, then I won't have a maid of honor. And no one can fit into your dress. I guess I'll just have to be nice to you for a few more weeks." Amy stood and filled a cup with coffee. "As long as you think there's still going to be a wedding. Otherwise I'm taking off for Australia and doing some crazy surfing."

"You know Justin would just come find you and drag you back." I studied my friend. She was solid. She'd get through this.

She set down her cup on the counter. "Then we'd better get these napkins folded. I've got too much still to do for the wedding, and the mayor wants me to put together a *Build Your Next Home in South Cove* pamphlet to hand out at the St Patrick's Day fair. Although I don't think we need more businesses and there isn't much room for another subdivision."

"The mayor is an insistent promoter." I set down my own cup, but it was empty anyway. "We still on for brunch tomorrow?"

"Sure. Why don't you bring Evie? She needs to get out of the apartment more." Amy glanced in the direction of Esmeralda's house. "Do you think Esmeralda would come?"

I shook my head as I focused on folding the napkin. "I'm going over this evening to chat, and to see how she's doing. I can ask, but I don't think she's even leaving the house now lately. Steve has her flustered."

Amy held up a hand. "Okay, don't shoot the messenger, but if Esmeralda didn't kill Nan, who did?"

"I'll assume your question is asked with good intentions. Honestly, I don't know. The motive is what we're missing. But I'd put more money on a crazy love triangle than the fortune-teller wanting her prediction to come true. That's just crazy. Maybe it was someone with a hidden meaning. Maybe it was a rival computer guy who was trying to leverage Steve and she was attacked after the guy followed her here?" I realized my theories were beginning to be a little conspiratorial.

Amy smiled at me. "That's what I love about talking with you. No theory is too far-fetched."

"The problem is every theory I come up with doesn't make sense and a lot of them support the public theory that Esmeralda killed Nan. So many people heard her complaining about her client going over the bend. She could have flipped from good to bad and back again without anyone knowing she had a change of heart." I sighed and smoothed the napkin fabric. This creative stuff just wasn't my bag. I knew people made money doing it, but I'd never be one of those artists who made jewelry or ... A thought hit me. I left the kitchen and ran to my office and picked up my laptop. When I came back Amy was staring at me like I'd lost my mind. I grinned at her. "I just remembered that Neal said Nan ran a home business. I wonder what she did. If she was a wedding planner, maybe one of her clients killed her to get her to stop making her fold napkins."

"Funny girl." Amy continued to work on the napkins as I started searching for Nan Gunter on the internet. "Are you finding anything?"

I'd started with Facebook. It was my go-to place to at least try to see what people were thinking. I might also use it as my news source, or at least a start. If something bad was happening in any part of the world, someone would mention it on Facebook. Then I could look at actual news outlets for the real facts. She had a profile, as did Steve. As I looked at joint friends, I noticed Neal's name on both my list and Nan's lists. I made a habit of friending all the new residents and business owners in town. It made it easier to follow up on Business-to-Business stuff if you could just message someone rather than sending an email.

She must have friended him after meeting him at the winery last week. So sad. I didn't try to friend Nan now as she would have had to approve it and, well, she couldn't. Then I noticed she had a business page. There were two actually. One was for Steve's computer company. He consulted for large companies on cybersecurity. That was interesting and a possible lead.

Then I went to Nan's business page. It was a full-on sales job. I glanced up at Amy and turned my laptop toward her. "This is interesting."

She read the page and scrolled down to a few of the posts. "She sold a day-trading class?"

"Sold and promised real money results. Maybe someone didn't like the no-money-back guarantee?" I copied the link and pasted it into an email to Greg. "He probably knows about this, but if there is at least one angry customer, it could take some of the heat off Esmeralda."

Amy glanced around at the napkin pile. Somehow, as we'd been chatting and talking, most of them were done. "Okay then, I think we've both had a busy day. Let's finish these up and I'll buy dinner."

"Let me text Greg to let him know I'll be out." I pulled out my phone from my pocket.

Amy stilled my hand. "You two didn't have plans, right? I don't want to be a third wheel."

"Are you kidding? He knows how to cook if he's coming home to eat. I think he's probably eating at the station tonight. He's shook up about Esmeralda's involvement in this murder. He wants the case solved as quickly as possible and to get her name cleared so she can come back to work. He leaned on her a lot. I think she'll be getting a raise when she comes back." I sent a quick message, then picked up a napkin. "Besides, he gets that we need friend time too."

"Greg's a keeper." Amy folded a napkin in half the time it had taken me. Which was fine; this wasn't a race, I told myself.

When we got to Diamond Lille's, Toby was already there and waved us over to his table. "Hey, guys. Great minds and all."

"Easy to do when there's only one full-menu restaurant in town," Amy reminded him.

"It's still nice to see you." He leaned forward. "Jill helped me take down the attacker at Esmeralda's."

"That's one way to put it." I grabbed his glass of water and took several sips from it. "You can have mine."

Toby waved Carrie over. "Hey, Princess, bring these two menus."

"Don't call me Princess." Something flashed in Carrie's eyes and I pulled back into the back of the booth. Maybe she wouldn't see me sitting there and only Toby would be in the doghouse for his choice of words. She selected menus from the hostess stand and slapped them on the table. "I'll be right back for your order."

I blinked and watched her storm away. "I don't think I've ever seen Carrie in a bad mood before."

Amy turned to Toby. "First for me. What did you say to her earlier?"

He ran a hand through his hair. "I don't remember. Something about being a long day, she agreed, took my order, and dropped off the food. She was normal then."

"Did one of the other customers get in her face about something?" I prodded.

Toby shook his head. "No. It's been quiet in here. You know I watch for those things. It's one of the first things you learn on the job that you are never really off the job. She dropped off my food. Oh, then Doc came in, they talked at the hostess stand, he got a call and left."

"Oh, Doc came in?" I settled back in the booth. Apparently, the lovebirds were fighting over something. One more piece of the puzzle that said they were in a relationship, even though both of them denied it.

Amy eyed me suspiciously. "And what are you not telling us?"

The table quieted as Carrie came back for our order. "Sorry I was a little snappy just now. Like Toby said, it's been a long day."

I told her what I wanted and Amy listed off her specific order trying to stay within some calorie count for the diet she didn't need. Then the door opened and Doc Ames walked back inside. I glanced at Carrie's face as she tried to keep it from showing any emotion, but I saw the hope jump in her eyes, just for a second.

Then a woman followed Doc in and they went to sit in a booth. As they passed by, Doc nodded a greeting. And Evie grinned at us.

"Hey, guys, I guess this is the place to be tonight." She laughed as she followed Doc to the booth.

Carrie put her fingers on the table, gripping it like she was about to pass out. Evie was at least thirty years younger than either Carrie or Doc. There was no way this was a date. But Carrie seemed to think it was. Her eyes met mine and I saw the hint of tears.

"If there's nothing else, I think it's time for my break. Debbie will bring out your food for you. Have a nice night." She spun around.

"Carrie, wait …" I called after her, but either she didn't hear me or she didn't want to stop. From the tilt of her head I wondered if she'd get out of the dining room before the tears fell.

Toby and Amy were staring at me now. "What's going on?"

I sighed and glanced over at the booth where Doc and Evie sat, talking. "Nothing good."

Chapter 12

Sunday mornings I sleep in. It's a law, at least in my house. It and Monday are the only two days I get off, so I make sure I turn off my alarm and sleep until my body wakes me up. Or the sun. Or Emma.

Today it was Greg and his bacon frying at seven in the morning that woke me and Emma. I heard her nails on the hard wood floor as she skittered downstairs to see if Greg was in a giving mood and she was going to get bacon for breakfast. My dog has an iron stomach and is able to eat most things, including the foam from my sofa pillows with no issues. We just try not to feed her a lot of human food, mainly for our peace of mind. What she eats on her own, well, we can't control that. I buy her expensive dog food to keep her healthy. Somedays I hope it counteracts all the nonfood substances she eats.

By the time I got downstairs Emma was outside. I glanced out the window to the backyard and found her playing catch by herself. She'd throw up the ball, then go chase it. It was cute to watch. "You must have given her a slice for her to be in that good a mood."

"She's my girl. You know I have a soft spot for your dog, right? If we ever break up, we have to set up a custody arrangement." He set a plate of scrambled eggs and bacon on the table at my spot and nodded to the fridge. "You want some OJ this morning?"

"Sure." I poured a cup of coffee and sat down, leaving my dog to her amusements. "You didn't have to cook. I've got a brunch date with Amy and Evie at eleven."

"I guess that will be more lunch than brunch then. Besides, I wanted to talk to you and I have to leave early, so this is my way of getting you out of bed early on a Sunday."

"Your evil plan can't work if you keep telling me your hidden agenda all the time." I took a slice of bacon and took a bite. Crunchy and brown to the point of almost being burned. It was yummy. "So, what do we need to chat about?"

"I was wondering if you talked to Esmeralda yesterday. She came down to the station to give a statement, but she's really shook up. I think this guy has her questioning her side business." He watched my face as I considered what I was going to say.

"Honestly, Amy had a wedding emergency, so I had to fold napkins and calm her down yesterday. I thought about stopping in, but by the time I got home from dinner, her lights were off. I figured she'd turned in early." I felt a pang of guilt for not going over to talk to my neighbor. What kind of a friend was I? Of course I'd been pulling Amy together, so I had a bit of an excuse.

"If you get a moment today, can you stop in and talk to her? I'm worried about her. She seems beat down. I know she didn't kill that woman and I'm going to find out who did. But for now, Esmeralda's getting the backlash from some town residents." He shook his head. "You wouldn't believe the calls I got yesterday. I can fight against hate crimes around race or sexuality, but when someone believes in a different manner about the other world? Now normal people feel like they're on some sort of religious crusade."

"God told them to be mean to Esmeralda?" I sipped my juice. This was getting out of hand.

"You can't suffer a witch or some crap." He glanced at his watch. "I'm meeting with Pastor Bill and his board, hoping to nip this anti-Esmeralda campaign in the bud. He called an emergency deacon meeting before services and I guess his sermon this week is on tolerance. I'm meeting with the leaders of the other two churches in town later today, so don't expect me until dinner."

"You're a good man. Thanks for sticking up for her. And thanks for breakfast." I put my hand his arm to stop him as he stood to take his plate to the sink.

He kissed me, then grinned. "Actually, if I was a really good man, I wouldn't leave you with the dishes, but I've got to get ready for church. Times three."

* * * *

I had some time before I went to Diamond Lille's to meet up with Amy and Evie. Glancing at the clock, I saw it was too early to make a visit to my neighbor. Instead, I pulled out my laptop and decided to find out more about Nan Gunter and her husband. Maybe that would help me identify a viable killer candidate because Greg didn't seem to think that Steve's having a mistress was enough of a motive. Emma curled up on the couch with me as I started the research. I'd go back to what Amy and I had found the day before. The businesses.

I found Steve's business first. It was a computer start-up that had an office just north of Bakerstown. I figured Steve must have worked from home because they'd said they were out of San Francisco, but when I looked at locations, I realized they had a satellite office near what was probably their hometown. I wrote down the town name and the Bakerstown address. I wasn't sure that a visit to the place would tell me much, but stranger things had happened. Maybe I'd take a drive out there on Monday. As I scrolled through the "About Us" tab, I found pictures of the management team. Steve was listed as owner and CEO. And down the page I saw Candice's picture as head of legal. So she was the company lawyer. Candice was pretty in a completely California surfer-girl style, her long, blond hair straight with highlights. She was the typical trophy wife type. After making notes about what I'd found, I went looking for Nan's digital footprint.

I found several Google hits that went to old blog posts about day trading. She had been active in the practice and had been a big supporter of the craft. Some of her blogs read more like infomercials about day trading and mentioned her online school. When I found the class link I blinked at the cost. Almost five thousand for a twenty-session class, along with access to a private Facebook page and a one-hour consultation session with Nan.

Testimonials filled the page, with students claiming to make their money back and more with only part-time work effort. One thing my aunt had always taught me was just because someone says it's true doesn't mean it is. And something we'd learned lately: Not everyone was who they said they were. I wondered if any of Nan's students' quotes were real. I couldn't access the Facebook page, but on a hunch I typed in complaints against Grow Rich Today, which was the name of Nan's company. It didn't take long for the hits to start building on my screen.

"There's the true story," I said as the list of hits continued to grow. Nan's proven technique didn't seem to be replicable and she had a ton of unhappy customers. I wondered if Greg had started to research the complaints. I wrote down what I could find, especially the ones with names and harsh complaints.

Then I closed the laptop. Who was I kidding? No one killed another person just because their training didn't work out. Did they? I ripped out the pages from my notebook, folded them in half, then wrote Greg's name on the top. I put the papers in the middle of the table. I'd let a real professional deal with this part of the investigation.

Time to get ready for brunch with the girls.

* * * *

When I left the house I'd taken a minute to cross the street and knock on Esmeralda's door. I'd been planning on inviting her to come to brunch with us. Either she was still sleeping or she was out. I didn't want to think that a third option might be the real truth: She didn't want to see me.

Amy and Evie were already at Diamond Lille's when I arrived. I hurried to the booth, glancing around to see if Carrie was working today. I put my tote on the bench next to Amy and stared at Evie. "You want to explain your dinner yesterday?"

She frowned and closed the menu. "Man, this is a small town. I can't believe the gossip train is already talking about who I'm having dinner with."

"I didn't get my information from the gossip train. Remember, I was here when you came in. Were you on a date with Doc?" I leaned closer so my voice wouldn't travel.

"What?" Evie's voice raised as mine lowered. "You thought that was a date?"

I glanced over and saw Carrie watching us. I nodded toward her. "No, but she did. She and Doc are, well, something, and it hurt her to see you with him."

"I just talked to him about the victim. I had a theory and wanted to run it past him. So I invited him to dinner. You don't think he thought it was a date, do you?" Evie glanced over at Carrie. "And that's his girlfriend? Whoa, I'm in a heap of trouble here, aren't I?"

I sighed. With the way rumors ran through South Cove, Evie could be considered a problem if we didn't nip this in the bud now. I didn't want to ruin my brunch with a scene, but if we could have a small one to keep the tension down, it would be worth it. I slipped out of the booth and headed over to Carrie.

When she saw me coming she turned her back and started setting up silverware behind the counter.

"Carrie?" I saw her shoulders twitch, but she pretended not to hear me. "Carrie, come on, I want you to meet Evie."

"Why would I want to meet his new girlfriend? I'm not that progressive. And I'm not fighting for the old coot. If he wants some young, beautiful woman, he's welcome to her." Carrie glanced over her shoulder at me. "This is where I work. Can you take her to eat somewhere else?"

"You need to listen to her side of the story. They didn't have a date last night. Evie's got the investigation bug from me. This is my fault."

Now Carrie did turn around. "They were talking about the murder?"

I nodded. "I took her to meet Doc a few days ago and we talked about the murder. Evie had a new theory she'd been working on and when she saw him in town, she figured she'd buy him dinner and pick his brain."

"Oh my. There's no fool like an old fool." Carrie snuck another glance at Evie. "I just thought because she was so pretty and they seemed to laugh a lot.... And, well, I didn't stick around to let him talk to me. I'd had a horrible day already, with Lille on my back for something I didn't even do. So I ran like a schoolgirl who had been jilted at the prom."

"I'm sorry you had a bad day, but you know how South Cove is. Come meet her. We need to get both of you out of the South Cove gossip spotlight. She's a nice person. She doesn't deserve to be villainized over this." I met Carrie's gaze. "Can we bury the hatchet and be friends?"

"You're always taking care of people. Have you ever thought that maybe adults can stand on their own two feet and fight their own battles?" Carrie smiled and patted my arm as she moved out from behind the counter.

"I just want people to be happy and to be friends. Especially my employees. That way they don't leave on me and cause a huge hole in scheduling."

Carrie laughed and then came over so I could introduce her to Evie.

Evie smiled. "I'm so happy to meet you. Everyone talks about how kind you are. Dr. Ames couldn't stop talking about you and your crafts last night."

Carrie smiled. "I should have stopped by your table then and met you. Sorry I didn't."

"No worries. I just didn't want there to be any confusion about my intentions with your beau. All I want from him are clues on how poor Ms. Gunter died. My boss here got me started trying to solve these investigations." Evie smiled at me. "Sometimes I just jump too far with my questions."

The open discussion seemed to calm Carrie down, and I noticed a lot of the townspeople seated in the diner were now smiling at Evie instead of the glares she'd been getting when I walked into the diner earlier. As we finished our meal, Evie leaned into me. "I swear, from now on I'm going to check with you before I talk to anyone about having even a coffee together." Laughing, I set down my iced tea. "It's not that bad here, really. It's just Carrie and Doc are at that strange part of the relationship where neither one has really admitted it, but everyone in town is rooting for them."

Amy ate her last bite of salad. "You'll figure out who's with who quickly. Townspeople see you as a possible threat for their favorite couples. We don't have a lot of single women. And I think it's sexist, but they look at you differently than a single man who lives in town. Toby hasn't had one spec of trouble, but he's Toby. It will get better as people start to know you."

"Well, I'm so glad you two asked me to lunch. I had already made my first gaffe and didn't even know it." Evie leaned back in the booth. "I did find out something from Dr. Ames you might find interesting."

"Okay, that's burying the lead, but what?" I leaned forward.

"The marks on her neck show strangulation. And the hands weren't big according to the prints. It could have been a woman."

Amy slapped the table. "Which goes with our mistress theory. I swear, your boyfriend better lock that one up before she decides to kill again."

"That's a little overdramatic, don't you think?" I pushed away my plate, unable to eat more. This investigation had me worried. Esmeralda needed to be out of the limelight. Greg needed her at the station. I'd never seen my neighbor so upset about something I knew she hadn't done. Now I just needed to prove it.

* * * *

When I woke the next morning Emma lay in Greg's spot. I checked the clock. It was after eight. I'd gotten my wish to sleep in. From the shape of the bed I assumed Greg had come home, but as usual during an investigation, he hadn't stayed long.

Downstairs, I let Emma out and sat down at the table with a notebook to make a list for the day. I had my share of housework to finish, but I wanted to learn more about Steve's business. I decided to make a quick run into town. I could buy pet food as my excuse; I hadn't stopped at the pet shop the last time I was in Bakerstown.

I hurried to get ready, then made sure all the doors were closed so Emma couldn't get into anything. If I hurried, I could be in and out before anyone even noticed I was gone. If Greg knew, he'd want to at least send someone with me, and Evie was working my shift this morning. Besides, I probably wouldn't even go inside. I'd just drive by to check the place out. When I got to the address I had to check my phone again: 4242 Skyline Way, Bakerstown. I was at the right place. But instead of an office building or even a remodeled house, the place was an abandoned farm. I parked and walked up to the mailbox. Dusting off the side, I verified the letters with the ones on my phone. This was the business address for Gunter Computer Solutions? I took several pictures, then, instead of getting back into my car, I walked up the overgrown dirt driveway.

The house used to be white, with an off white picket fence around it. It was small, maybe eight hundred square feet and two story. Broken windows let the wind play with old, rotting curtains that flowed with the gentle breeze. I walked around the house and saw a storm cellar near an old clothesline. And in the back, a large barn sat, massive, in the yard. The large doors were open and I could see some hay bales and an old tractor. This wasn't a swank office building for a computer consulting company. This was a piece of abandoned property waiting for someone to tear everything down and build something new. I glanced around but didn't see anything that would tell me why this was listed as the corporate office address.

I got back into the car and pulled up the website on my phone. Same address. I checked the map app to see if there were any office buildings nearby, but the closest commercial building I saw was a drive-in near Highway 1. I glanced at my watch. It was almost lunchtime.

I took it as a sign.

Chapter 13

After running with Emma when I got home, I walked back to the house. Esmeralda sat on her porch. I crossed the road and sat on the swing. "How are you doing?"

"I'm fine. Look, I'm not crazy. I didn't kill Nan, no matter what Steve thinks. I just felt like Greg was going to have enough on his plate without having to stand up for the local witch." She pushed her mop of curly hair from her face and twisted it into one lock that she tied into a low knot on the back of her head. The change made her look younger. More vulnerable. "Rory, Deek's mom, is coming over tonight and we're drinking and talking until we pass out on the floor. You're welcome to join us."

"As fun as that sounds, I have a feeling Greg might be home tonight. He's been gone so much lately that I'd like us to spend some time together if possible. But if he calls and tells me to eat on my own, I'll come over." I scratched my dog behind her ears. Emma leaned her head on my lap, her gaze finding my own. She was easy to please. "I can't believe Steve is still so upset. You'd think he'd realize you didn't kill Nan."

"He needs someone to blame besides himself. He told me that he was trying to stop her from coming here. That he'd had a bad feeling lately. He must have thought she was going a bit mad without their son." She leaned her arms on her thighs. "I can't say I blame her."

"What do you know about her business? Did she have people threatening her about the product?" Esmeralda probably knew more about these people than anyone else. I might as well use my source.

"She said there was a fool born every minute and she had the business to prove it." Esmeralda leaned her head back. "I knew she was cheating people. Selling hope. It never turns out well when all you want is the money."

I didn't want to point out that she was also in the hope business, but she probably had a better heart and wanted people to heal, not hurt. "You're saying she knew her training wasn't teaching people a skill?"

"She said day trading was nothing but gambling. She was making money on the system she sold, not as a trader. Steve built her website and helped her set up the training. He's good with computers." Esmeralda stroked Emma's head as she spoke.

"Did he say where his office was?" My dog liked calming people. And she was good at it.

"He worked out of his house. I guess they were going to build an office, but once they lost Eric, he lost interest."

And now the property made sense. I guessed there wasn't a wild story about it. I'd wasted most of my day going to look at an old house. I glanced at my watch. I still had time to get home and take a shower before getting dinner started. "I guess I'd better get home. I'm glad Rory is coming over tonight."

Esmeralda nodded. "Me too. Rory and I grew up together. There's no one who has more dirt on me or knows how to get me out of a funk. It's good to have girlfriends you can count on. Like you and Amy. How's the wedding planning going?"

"Fine. I just hope everything goes as planned this time. I don't think she could deal with another delay. And Justin's being weird. But maybe that's just being a groom. Getting these two married might be the death of me." I stood up, and Emma came to stand next to me. "If you need me, you know where to find me."

"I do. And I appreciate you checking in on me. You're a good neighbor, Jill."

As we walked across the street and into the backyard gate, I wondered if I *was* a good neighbor. Maybe I should have agreed to go to the party. On the other hand, I would have felt like an outsider, being with two old friends like that. I unlocked the back door. "You don't have to save the world, Jill."

Maybe not, but it was nice to know there were others out there, like Rory, to pick up some of the slack.

As I'd assumed he would, Greg came home for dinner. Esmeralda would have said I was using the gift I didn't like to acknowledge, but really, I knew I was working from his pattern. There was a point in all the investigations at which he'd followed all the leads, put out all the feelers, and still nothing was working. That was when he came home to relax and let his mind work. I'd heard authors talk about the same thing. They called it writer's block. When the story was just hiding from you. But I figured this was more like letting a stew cook. He needed his thoughts to simmer. And I needed to bug him to tell me bits and pieces about the investigation. Even though, as he told me often enough, I wasn't a trained investigator. I pulled out the roasted chicken to check for doneness, then the potatoes. I should be able to pull it all together in the next thirty minutes.

Greg stopped in the doorway to the kitchen after coming in the front and being attacked by Emma. She'd missed him. He took in a deep breath. "Jill, you are an angel. I don't think I could take another night of pizza—not even Tiny's special. The guys are on a pizza kick lately. I actually added a side salad to the order last night just to have something different."

"Go get a shower and dinner will be ready right at six. That way if something happens, you'll be ready to leave." I stepped over to give him a kiss. Afterward I leaned my head into his chest. "I've missed you."

"And I you. Not to ruin the mood, but have you talked to Esmeralda lately? She won't answer my calls and there's a Mercedes in the driveway now, so I didn't want to bother her." He rubbed my back.

Stepping away from the hug I didn't want to end, I went back to the stove to dump the water from the potatoes. The steam felt warm on my face. "That's her friend, Rory. She's Deek's mom. They're doing a girls' night."

"That makes me feel better. So she's okay?"

I considered his question. "She's worried about perception. It's not that she wanted to leave. Somehow she knew the town would turn on her with this murder."

"The whole town isn't turning, just some bigoted few," he corrected me as he stood staring into the fridge. "Besides, someone came in with an alibi for her on Doc's estimated time of death for Nan."

"Wasn't it late Tuesday?" I wondered who would have been with Esmeralda that late. Another client?

"Ten thirty, give an hour or two either way. We were there from eight to nine and she was alive. So that takes the other end up to midnight, more or less. And Esmeralda had an overnight guest who is totally credible."

"Her friend Rory?"

Greg grinned. "Nope. Not a friend. Or not just a friend. He says they've been seeing each other for a few months now. He's from New Orleans and they were tight growing up."

"Nic something? She told us about him at the haunted house getaway." I glanced toward Esmeralda's house. "He was there all night?"

"Again, not for the rumor mill, but yes." Greg leaned on the wall, watching me cook. "I'm happy she has someone in her life. I didn't know she was seeing someone long distance."

"Well, that explains her trips to New Orleans this last year. I thought she was doing some marketing stuff for her business. Maybe learning new woo-woo techniques? But a boyfriend. Man, I wish I'd known this earlier. I might have been able to find out more about him."

"Don't go prodding. This is for your ears only. I just wanted to let you know that she has an alibi. Unless he did the murder with her; then I have a bigger problem because I liked the guy." Greg rolled his shoulders. "Now that Esmeralda's officially off the list, I can work on a new suspect."

"Great, who's that?" I added butter and milk to the drained potatoes and went to find my hand mixer.

"I'll tell you as soon as I know."

I didn't get the chance to ask him about Steve's side piece before he took off upstairs. I'd bring up the subject and the corporate headquarters thing at dinner. I started humming as I beat the potatoes to a nice whip. Then I made gravy. The day had just gotten a little brighter.

* * * *

When I got to the shop the next day Darla was sitting at the doorway. Again. Stifling an inward groan, I pasted on a smile and opened the door. "You want some coffee?"

"Yes, please. And I want to know what you found out this weekend. I tried calling you several times, but your phone went to voice mail." Darla followed me into the dining room.

I flipped on the lights and the room glowed to life. It made me happy each and every morning when I did that. I guess it's the little things. "My bad. I left my phone in my purse and it went dead. I'm so bad at charging it now that I'm not Jackie's emergency contact. Although I guess anything could happen. I need to be more diligent."

"And you're avoiding my question. What did you find out this weekend?" Darla pressed as she climbed up on a stool and pulled out her notebook. She held her pen poised over the paper and watched me.

I ignored her pointed stare. "I have to get coffee going first. Just hold on."

She waited a good five minutes, then, as I was stacking cups in the fifth pile on the counter, she groaned. "You're stalling. What is it you can't tell me?"

"I don't know." I gave up on the obvious stall technique because she'd called me out and poured our coffees. Then I went around the counter and sat down. "What do you know about the investigation?"

"I know that crazy man tried to break into Esmeralda's house. Twice. He must have some high-powered attorney because he was out by the end of the day. Is it true she decided not to press charges? I'd say the woman was a saint if she didn't do that fortune-telling stuff." Darla sipped her coffee. "And I heard a rumor that she's been pretty much cleared of the killing. Some mystery man with an alibi?"

"That's what I heard too. And no, I don't have anything else on that." I thought about the abandoned farmhouse. "I went to Steve's corporate office north of Bakerstown yesterday."

Darla's eyes went wide. "I should have thought of that. What did they say? Did anyone talk to you? If you'd taken me, we could have used my press pass for more push on the interview. You are just a civilian, even though everyone in South Cove knows you have Greg's ear."

"Maybe I have his ear, but he's not happy when he gets information from me. He says I'm going to get myself hurt one of these days. I guess he's right, but I couldn't let Esmeralda go down for something she didn't do." I sipped my coffee.

"And now that she's cleared? Are you done investigating? Is that what you've been keeping from me?" Darla fixed me with a look. I knew what it meant. Was I caving under Greg's pressure to stay out of it?

"No. Now I just want to know who killed Nan. If I can help put her killer behind bars, well, that's my good deed for the day. Or maybe the year." I smiled as I glanced around the still-empty coffee shop. Last week townsfolk had been piling in just to hear the scoop. Today, even my commuters were absent. Of course Tuesday was typically slow with commuter traffic. They were still excited about the workweek. Tomorrow would be a madhouse.

"So, you didn't tell me. What did the corporate goons say? Or did they hide behind their lawyer?" Darla's eyes were bright. There was a reason she wrote for the paper; she loved the hunt for a good story. I often wondered if she'd really wanted to be a writer rather than take on her parent's winery when they retired.

"Hello, Jill?" Darla's voice broke through my thoughts.

"Sorry, woolgathering." I sipped my coffee. Then I picked up my phone and showed her the pictures. "There are six there. Keep scrolling."

She followed my instructions, then went back and looked more slowly this time. She handed my phone back. "I don't understand."

"Neither do I. But that's the address listed on the website for the corporate office. According to Esmeralda, Steve works out of his home office. And they were planning on building an office, but when their son died the plans got delayed." I held up a finger as a customer came into the shop. "Hey, Tori, your usual?"

"Black, hot, and huge." The woman winked at Darla. "Just don't tell my doctor. I told him I was giving up caffeine last week. They think I'm working too hard and the coffee keeps me going."

"Now I'm contributing to your addiction." I filled the order and took her card. "Maybe we should try half decaf tomorrow?"

"Now where's the fun in that?" She signed her receipt and handed it back to me. "Maybe a quarter decaf. I need it to taste great."

"It will, I promise." I put the charge slip into the drawer and waited for Tori to leave.

"That must be hard to hear," Darla said, stirring her new favorite drink with fewer calories.

"No, I believe people are adults. I can suggest things, but if you need a slice of cheesecake or a large cup of coffee to get through the day? That's on you. Besides, we go through this every month. She's been on three quarters decaf for two months now. She just doesn't know it. And she gets to think she's fooling her doctor." I smiled at the door where Tori had disappeared. "Last month she came in and told me her blood pressure had gone down enough the doctor was thinking about taking her off her meds."

"You're selling her a fake coffee?" Darla looked at me like I'd admitted there was no Santa Claus.

"No, I'm following her directions. She came in six months ago and told me her doctor said she couldn't drink coffee at all. Then we agreed I'd put a quarter decaf in the cup. Each month we've had the same conversation, I up the decaf bit by bit. She only drinks my coffee, and my decaf is almost as good as my regular. She gets what she needs and I'm just following her instructions. She just doesn't remember giving them to me."

"It's still sneaky. When are you going to tell her she's been drinking decaf?" Darla finished her coffee and stood.

"Maybe when her doctor takes her off the meds. If she's healthy, maybe she'll let me stop." I shrugged. "Or maybe not. Everyone has at least one downfall. Hers is coffee. Mine is good food. That's why I run."

"I'm not a runner, but Matt has me working out with him. It's cute the way he tries to show me how to lift more and more weight. I enjoy being part of something he loves." Darla checked her watch. "And that's where I'm heading next. I'll give this corporate office address a run through my computer searches. Maybe the guy he got it from is mad, or maybe the developer. Losing a contract of that size could cause someone to kill. Money is always a factor in bad decisions."

"Let me know what you find out," I called as I nodded to the next commuter. It was time for me to put away my amateur detective role and play barista and bookstore expert. Some of my commuters were my best book buyers.

Today I was working a longer shift to get things organized for our St. Patrick's Day Street Fair on Friday and Saturday. I was setting up a book booth with Deek on Irish and Irish American authors, as well as books about Ireland. And Evie was in charge of a special Make Yourself a Leprechaun craft table inside in the children's book section. It should be a fun day. We were running the kids' section until five; then she was taking off for the city and Olivia's party.

The book booth would close up at eight. I was working the full day on Saturday, but I'd assigned Evie my next Tuesday shift to kind of make up for it. In between commuters I started to make my to-do list and set up plan. Typically, Jackie did this kind of planning work, but she'd asked me to handle this one. I figured she thought I really didn't know how, so this would be a good learning experience for when she left the business and started traveling full-time. My aunt forgets I ran the business for five years before she came to help for a week and never left. Or she was just enjoying spending more time with Harrold, her new husband. It was nice seeing my aunt happy. Maybe after Amy and Justin said the "I do's," Amy would be less stressed too.

As if I'd called her by thinking about her, Amy walked through the front door and burst into tears. I left the counter and ran over to her. "What's wrong?"

"Justin just called and said he was delayed. Then we got cut off." Amy sniffed. "It sounded like he was in an airport. What would he be doing in an airport?"

The last time I'd talked to Justin he was still planning their honeymoon. Maybe he'd taken a trip to check a place out? He was a pretty thorough researcher. But I couldn't say that to Amy. She'd freak out knowing he hadn't booked a resort yet. "I told you he said he had to go to Nebraska to see his mom."

Amy stopped sobbing and looked at me. She frowned as she wiped her eyes. "Oh, that's right. I was going to ask him about that, but I never seem to have the time. He would have tried to keep something like that from me because I told him he needed to be close for last-minute decisions. It would be just like him to go around me on this. He hates conflict."

"See, there's no need for tears. He'll be here on the day that matters. Your wedding day." I put my arm around her and led her to the counter.

"Why don't you have a slice of lime cheesecake? Sadie made it special for the street fair this weekend. And brownies with green mint cream cheese threaded through them."

Amy glared at me like I'd slapped her. "Are you crazy? I can't eat something like that. I'd gain ten pounds just smelling the sugar."

I kind of thought that was impossible, but I wasn't going to argue with the bridezilla who'd taken over my friend's body. "Okay then. What about a nice cup of soothing tea? Or maybe some coffee?"

"Coffee. Large, black to go. I have to go back to City Hall before Mayor Baylor finds me gone. The man is convinced he can't answer his own calls. And now that Esmeralda isn't there, it's all me. I hope she comes back before my honeymoon or Greg's going to have to assign Toby or Tim to be a part-time dispatcher and receptionist."

"There are such things as temp agencies, you know. I bet you could get someone to come in and work until she comes back." I poured the coffee and set it in front of my friend.

Amy tried to hand me cash, but I shook my head.

"On the house."

She nodded. "Thanks, but I don't want anyone to get the idea Esmeralda is actually gone and the position is open. She needs to come back and I don't want anyone to think she's easily replaced."

After Amy left I thought about her words. I hoped Esmeralda came back sooner rather than later, mostly for Greg's benefit. Because if she didn't, he would have to replace her. And that wouldn't be good for anyone, including Esmeralda.

Chapter 14

When Deek arrived we gathered to finish the planning for Saturday's event. Evie volunteered to handle the customers, so the rest of us sat in the office around the mess that was my work desk. Or Aunt Jackie's desk. It belonged to whoever last sat at it.

Deek had already ordered the books and was unboxing and stacking them in specific piles near the walk-in cooler. I needed to run to Bakerstown to get some festive supplies because we couldn't find the box that held what we hadn't used last year. I made a list of items and kept adding to it as we talked. Green napkins, green plates, green cups, and green face paint for the kids. As well as green beads and hats. I thought I'd grab some of the fake crowns too, for the leprechaun princesses who may attend the event. I added a quick note to remind myself to make a kit for Olivia too. Evie could deliver it with my birthday gifts.

"You're lost in thought today," Deek observed as he made a planogram for the bookshelves we were moving outside for the fair. We'd bought some with rollers last year that, when we weren't having sidewalk events, could be scattered around the dining room or even tucked away by a wall. We were getting better at this festival mentality of selling anywhere and everywhere. A process that was helping our bottom line, which then allowed me to pay better wages. "Earth to Jill: Did you even hear me?"

I shook my head. "Sorry. Thinking about the festival and the shop and the past and the future. It's running together for me today. I don't know why I'm so lost in memories and what ifs."

"You don't like change." Deek's flat statement surprised me.

"What's change got to do with it?" I put down my pen and watched him as he changed the adult fiction books to the top of the plan and put the kids' books near the bottom. All the better to be grabbed by excited, tiny fingers. He knew his marketing. "There's just a lot going on right now."

"You can't blame your mood on the festival. You know it's just another day at work for you. No, this is about that lady's murder. You're worried." He frowned as he put memoirs over travel books, then erased the words and reversed them.

"I've been involved with investigations before. There's nothing new about that. So no, I'm not responding to change." My voice held a touch of edge to it that I didn't like. I leaned back in my chair and dropped my pen on my notebook. "Sorry. I'm grumpy too."

"You have been involved in investigations before, but not one when a friend is accused of the crime." He turned the plan around and showed it to me. "Does this look right? Should the travel books be on the bottom?"

"Nope. They're impulse buys. A customer needs them at eye level so they see it and think, 'I should go to Ireland someday. Maybe I'll buy the book and plan my escape.'" I pointed to the memoirs. "Those readers are going to actually come looking for the book. Less of an impulse buy."

"Good point." He went over and picked out a few of the books. "Did you see what I bought for the event? I hope most of it sells or we'll be sending a ton back to the publisher."

"I think we'll sell a lot this weekend. People are curious about their holidays." I initialed the plan, a step my aunt had implemented a few years ago so she knew someone besides the part-time employee planning the event had looked at it. I think she just wanted to control things, even when she didn't care about what was really happening. "Why would this investigation be different?"

"You don't want anything to happen to Esmeralda. My mom's torn up about this too. You probably know she spent the night over there. She didn't even tell me what I could do in the house or who I could invite over. She just packed an overnight bag and left. I think she's staying tonight too. She said Esmeralda is hurting." Deek repacked a box, then started a new stack of extras so they would be easy to find on festival day.

"What do you know about this Nic guy that Esmeralda is seeing? Is he reliable?"

Deek laughed. "From the stories my mom tells about when they all ran together, hell no. But they have a code. They protect one another."

"Might he lie for her?"

My question shocked Deek for a second, but he gave it some time before he answered. "To Greg? Might, yes. They don't have a real connection or love of law enforcement. But would he? I don't think so. Again, they have this honor thing going on. If Nic says he was with Esmeralda the night that lady was killed, he was there. I'd bet my life on it. Besides, he wouldn't want to do anything to get Esmeralda in trouble. If Nic even thought Esmeralda could be guilty, she'd already be set up in a new home on some tropical island."

I trusted my barista, but sometimes adults didn't tell the kids everything. "I am worried about Esmeralda. The town has turned on her. And there aren't a lot of clues pointing to the person who actually killed Nan."

He went back to the boxes for more books and laid them out on the table. Setting them up to show me the books he'd chosen. He paused, looking at me thoughtfully. "In books they always tell you to follow the money. Maybe it will work in real life too?"

* * * *

I made a folder with all the plans for Saturday and put it near the cash register for Aunt Jackie's review. I'd say something trite like she wasn't the boss of me, but we all knew it wasn't true. My aunt ruled her life and the lives of her subjects with an iron hand. The only sign of relief was that now she had Harrold. He kept her too busy to meddle too much in my life. On the other hand, I kind of missed her. I made a mental note to invite her over for dinner once this investigation was over and Greg had his life back.

I stopped at Diamond Lille's for a salad, but instead of eating in, I took it to go. Then I went and got Emma and filled a tote with my lunch, waters, a soda, and a book. I was going to go sit on the beach with my dog and eat. Then I'd spend the rest of the time reading. No running today. Our afternoon was going to be pure relaxation.

As we walked toward the picnic tables the town had set up near the parking area, I realized Esmeralda and Rory were walking toward me. Arm in arm like old friends, they were laughing. Their hair was blowing in the wind. The scene would have been a perfect picture. I paused before turning to the picnic area and waited for them to approach. Emma sat by my leg, her tail wagging and throwing sand. I'd worn capris that day, so the sand was stinging my leg as it hit. My dog has a strong wag.

"Jill, what a lovely surprise. It's a great day to spend your afternoon on the beach. Not too hot, not too cold." Esmeralda glanced around the empty beach. "Goldilocks weather."

Rory laughed at the reference. "You're spot-on. Jill, I'm not sure if you remember me; I'm Deek's mom."

"Of course. Deek speaks highly of you." I kept a tight grip on Emma's leash as a flock of seagulls landed right on the shoreline. Emma didn't like birds hanging out on her beach.

The easy laugh came again and I thought I could be friends with this woman. "He should. I've been supporting his education habit for too many years now. But finally I believe he's found his path."

"As long as he lets it go when it's done," Esmeralda warned. "The muse doesn't like for a story to sit and bubble too long. It needs to be out in the world, helping others."

"Esmeralda, I truly think this is his calling. I did a reading for him yesterday. Of course he doesn't think it's anything but a mothers' interference or wishful thinking, but the cards are supporting him being successful in his life plan." Rory stared at the crashing waves, seeming to be thinking of either Deek's future or her last reading.

"All I'm saying is, he needs to be prepared to actually work and act on his dreams." Esmeralda hugged her friend. "You're not the only one who is invested in Deek's future. I've been running tarot spreads on him since he was born."

"I know. You're a good godmother."

The conversation had gone from normal to odd in just a few minutes. I decided to use my lunch as an excuse to exit it. "Well, it was nice to see you both."

"Jill, I wanted to thank you for your support these last few weeks. It means a lot that even though you don't agree with my gifts—or your own, for that matter—that you're willing to back me when I fall into trouble."

"No worries. I know you didn't kill Nan. Even if you didn't have an alibi, it's just not in your DNA."

She studied me closely. "I'm not sure that's exactly true. I'm not an angel, Jill. I've done some bad stuff in my life."

"When you were a kid and under a bad influence." Rory patted her arm. "You need to forgive yourself for those actions. You weren't responsible."

"Even as a kid I knew right from wrong. That's why I left the family. Why I moved out here. I needed a clean break. I would have gone farther west, but I don't walk on water." Esmeralda glanced out over the ocean. "Maybe someday I'll go even farther. Hiding away so the past doesn't come back to bite me."

I didn't know her past except she'd been a foster kid and adopted by a wealthy and influential New Orleans family. The family who taught her how to read cards and people. I suspected there was a little bit of grift in her new family tree, but I'd never worried about Esmeralda. I trusted her.

She had a key to my house. I just hoped some rabid prosecutor wouldn't find the mistakes of her past and use her childhood against her. "I've always heard you can't run from your problems because everywhere you go, you're still there."

"Very true." Rory turned to me and studied me closely. "You're not just Deek's boss, you're also Esmeralda's neighbor, right? The one who lives with the cop?"

"That's me, Jill Gardner."

"Oh, is my face red. I didn't put the two names together until now. I used to live in the city, so having two Jills in your life wouldn't have even been an issue." Rory glanced at Esmeralda and something passed between them.

Something I was pretty sure was about me. I didn't push. Sometimes I just didn't want to know what others thought of me. It kept my spirits up. "Well, I'd really better get started on my lunch."

"Oh, yes, sorry, we didn't mean to hold you up so long." Rory bubbled as she talked. A light personality compared to Esmeralda's dark, muddled tones. "I'm sure we'll meet again."

"That would be nice. Maybe we'll have dinner next time you're in town?" I left the invitation open and started moving toward the picnic tables. "See you both later."

"You are looking in the wrong place. Family doesn't do this to each other. You need to follow the money," Esmeralda said.

I turned around, narrowing my eyes. "What did you say?"

She shook her head. When she saw my face her lips turned into a smile. "Go eat, Jill. I swear, you must be starving. Your face is as white as a ghost."

I glanced at Rory, who was staring at her friend too. Apparently, one of Esmerelda's spirit guides had come to visit. She shrugged as she followed Esmeralda toward the parking lot. I'd have to reach out to Deek later to see what message his mother had for me. Instead of making a big deal of it, I moved to the tables and sank down on one bench. I didn't know if I could get back up, my legs were shaking so hard.

I mean, I've been part of Esmeralda's magic before. She'd told me things under a glassy-eyed stare, then hadn't remembered what she'd said. But this time? The message seemed ominous. A message that needed to be heeded.

I pulled out my phone and tried to type into the notes section exactly what she'd said. The process wasn't easy because my fingers were shaking, and I had to keep going back to change my note just for it to make sense. When I was done I leaned back and read the note again. It wasn't about family. If I believed Esmeralda's spirit visitor, Steve didn't do it. Deek had said the same thing about following the money. I think having the same message twice had to mean something important. Since Nan's son died, the only family they'd had was each other.

Or was it?

I tied Emma to the table and opened my lunch, watching the waves while I ate. Emma laid down by my foot and did the same. Well, watched the waves and the seagulls. I tried to clear my head of all things about Nan's murder. Sometimes doing that let me come at it a different way when I focused again. I glanced at the book that was sitting next to my cardboard takeout bowl. And the best way to get out of my head was to get into a book. I needed to have a wide assortment of books read before my next staff recommends column was due, and I'd been spending my reading time trying to investigate Nan's murder.

It was time for me to put back on my business owner hat and leave the investigation to the professionals. I texted Greg the message that Esmeralda's spirit world friend had sent me, then I opened the book and got lost in the story.

March on a California beach sounds like a lovely place, but today was chilly and windy. After a few chapters I decided to take the reading time home to my couch, where I could throw a blanket over me and slip off my shoes. Emma got up from her spot, where she'd been watching seagulls, and after gathering our stuff into a tote we walked home.

The farmers market at the bottom of the hill and across the street from the beach was closed. The farm that owned it typically started the spring with open hours on the weekend. I was surprised when I saw Mandy Jensen get out of her car.

Instead of heading straight home, I aimed for the market parking lot and called out a greeting.

"Hey, Jill. How have you been?" She set the box she had gotten out of the truck onto the tailgate.

"Great. Are you getting ready for the St. Patrick's Day festival?" I pointed to Emma and she sat next to me, watching the newcomer.

"Getting our Irish on. We'll have a lot of green veggies for the day. I hope people stop by on their way up to Main Street. I always worry about sales the first few months of the season."

I frowned. "You're doing fine, right?"

"Definitely. I'm just a worrier." She leaned against the truck. "I have to say I'm not sorry Josh and I missed the paint-and-sip event. We had to run up to the farm to talk to my uncle about something. Then, the next morning, I heard about the woman who was killed. Can't say I'm surprised."

"That's right, Meredith said you two were coming. I'm sorry you didn't make it." Her words had shocked me. "So, why weren't you surprised? Did you know her?"

"I didn't, no. My friend's husband spent a lot of money on her course and lost a ton of his retirement funds on day trading. Fifty thousand gone in less than six months. Man, Anna was steamed. She told him he was stupid, and if he ever did something that risky again, she'd leave him." Mandy hefted a box from the trunk and stacked it near the shed's door. "It's hard to resist when you're promised such easy money, though. And she played with the fact he was smart. Book smart, with no common sense. I've heard people have tried to sue her, but she's got, or had, a really good lawyer. All the training says that results could vary."

"I'm sorry about your friend. Will they be okay?"

Mandy nodded. "The good thing is, she's a lawyer. She makes good money, but you know how expensive it is to live here. They'll rebound. I just feel bad for the ones who don't. The good news is the training course is down off the website now. I guess without Nan Gunter to push it, the family must have decided it wasn't worth the risk."

We said our goodbyes, and I thought about this new information. Money as a motive had come to me three times today from three different sources. If that wasn't a sign, I don't know what else I'd need to recognize it. I got settled on the couch after I'd made a promise to Google the business again to see if there were any reviews that might be perceived as a threat. Or maybe something on the Facebook page for the business. I couldn't see Nan's personal page because we weren't friends, but the other page was open.

I opened my book and tried to read. But Esmeralda's message kept coming back to me. Who was in Nan's family? I opened the laptop and started searching.

A loud knock on the door pulled me out of the research. Before I opened the door I glanced out the window. Amy stood there, a bag of food from Diamond Lille's in her hands and tears running down her face.

Chapter 15

"What on earth is wrong?" I asked as soon as I unlocked the door and swung it open.

Amy brushed past me. "I brought enough food in case Greg comes home for dinner, but is it okay if I hang with you tonight?"

"Of course." I relocked the door and followed my friend into the kitchen. Emma had already beat me there as food smells beat protect-the-owner instincts every time. When I reached the kitchen she had already unloaded a basket of fried chicken, mashed potatoes, rolls, coleslaw, and what appeared to be a French silk pie. One of my favorites. This was one of my favorite comfort food meals because it always reminded me of Sunday dinner with my aunt and her first husband, Ted. They'd both worked in food service, so cooking when they got home hadn't been a treat but instead was more like a chore. We did carryout every Sunday from the time I moved in with them as a kid until I left for college. They might have continued the tradition eventually, but Uncle Ted hadn't lasted much longer after I'd left home.

I knew emotional eating, and my friend was experiencing it. Amy typically only ate to fuel her active lifestyle. This was eating to quiet something inside. I took her arm and sat her down in a chair. I sat too, then focused on her. "What's wrong?"

"I still can't reach Justin. I know he's at his folks', but can't he just pick up the freaking phone? I know it hasn't been that long, but we've been inseparable for months. Now, a few weeks before our wedding, he goes dark on me? Ghosts me? Maybe his mother hates me." Amy sank into her chair.

I could tell she'd been crying, but it looked like the tears had dried up. Now she was just trying to survive. I didn't know what to say, but I knew how to be there for my friend. "Look, we both know Justin is crazy in love with you. If he's not picking up, he has a good reason. I think you need to relax. Give him some space. Worry about the upcoming nuptials. Is there anything you're missing?"

"You mean besides the groom?"

When I didn't react to her, she sighed and shook her head. "No. For once it's done. Everything's ready for me to walk down the aisle in a week and four days and join my life with another's."

"Then let's just get to that day. Justin will be here. If he doesn't show, we'll deal with it then. For right now, you need to have faith in him. In you two as a couple. He would give you the same leeway if you had to have a few days." I tried to think of positive excuses for why he wasn't calling her. I was going to have a long talk with him when he got back. By not telling her the Nebraska story, he'd put me in a bad situation

Amy closed her eyes and took in a few deep breaths. I figured she'd learned the technique in some yoga class. Amy loved yoga. I, on the other hand, always felt like I wasn't quite doing it right. Except for corpse pose. That one I could nail. Finally, she opened her eyes and wiped her cheeks with both hands to clear up any tears. "You're right. You're always right. I can't believe how calm you've been this, entire time even though you were probably going through some things too."

"That's what friends do. We help each other get through the dark times. Let's change the subject. Is City Hall having a table at the St. Patrick's Day Street Fair?"

"You bet we are. The police station is handing out toy badges for all the kids who stop by. I'll have a town sign-up for the city newsletter. And Mayor Baylor is partnering with the fire department to do home alarm checks. A firefighter will come to your home, check your alarms, and make suggestions for upkeep and repair. I guess he got a grant from the local hardware store in Bakerstown for man-hours as long as the guy points the homeowner his way when they got done. It's a win-win for the town." Amy's face had brightened a bit. "Justin told me he was going to help me man the booth on Saturday. Do you think I should replace him?"

I was torn. "Maybe have someone on standby just in case you haven't heard from him yet. You don't want to be upset when you try to find help."

"You're right. I have a list of volunteers just for this type of thing. I'm going to call one in the morning. That way if Justin does come home, we can have some quiet time to talk about what happened."

Man, I really didn't want to be Justin during that talk. Amy could be direct and to the point. And if Justin had forgotten about the commitment, Amy wouldn't mince her words, even for her fiancé. Maybe especially because he was her fiancé. I stood and took out some plates from the cupboard. "Amy, you need to realize that Justin is under as much pressure as you are. He's never been married before, and once he says his vows he'll take them seriously. That's who he is. He'd never do anything to directly hurt you."

She took the plate I handed her and nodded. "You're right. I'm being controlling. Are you sure you don't want to wait for Greg before we eat?"

I sat and opened the basket with the chicken. The warm aroma engulfed me and almost made me want to cry. I loved it when food was part of the story of why the world was the way it was. Food didn't wash away the bad in the world, but good food gave you the strength to get through a bad patch. Or maybe that was just me. "I'll text him and let him know we're eating. I'm sure if he's hungry, he'll be here. Especially if I say it's Tiny's secret recipe."

"Jill, you're mean." Amy laughed as she filled her plate.

I shook my head as I finished the text to Greg. "He'll be here as soon as he can get here." I heard the car door slam out in the driveway. "And maybe we caught a break. It sounds like I didn't even need to alert him to dinner."

"You don't mind if I still stay over even if he's home for the night?" Amy looked crushed at the fact that I might send her packing. But real friends didn't do that to each other.

"Of course not. You can come over any time. I get to keep my friends. We talked about this before we moved in together. Although I don't think he invites his guys over for football as much as I have people over. Maybe I should remind him it's his home too." I stood and grabbed another plate.

"Or maybe after being with the guys all day he'd rather come home and be with you." Amy smiled. "Greg's happy. You're happy. I wouldn't worry about the trappings."

By the time Greg had come inside I'd realized we needed a fourth plate. Toby had come to eat dinner with us. I liked having a full table. So many times it had been just me and Aunt Jackie for meals. Now I had friends and family to break bread with. And the situation filled my heart and soul with joy.

"Are you ready for the St. Patrick's festival?" Toby asked in between bites of chicken. "Greg has me on patrol all weekend so Deek's taking my shifts. I hope that's okay."

"We have Evie to fill in too." I took a bite of the mashed potatoes. It was my favorite side dish with everything. It didn't matter what the main course was, mashed potatoes should be the side. No questions asked. "We'll be fine."

Toby nodded. "I gave her a present for Miss Olivia this afternoon. And made my excuses."

"You are working the festival that day. It's a valid reason for not attending." I watched as Toby wiped his hands on his napkin.

"Yeah, but you know it's not the real reason. Sasha will too. When we were together I would have moved heaven and earth to attend Olivia's birthday, even if I had to work triple shifts to free up some time." He took another piece of chicken from the basket. "Now I'm out of the picture, and soon she won't even know who the gifts are from. I guess that will be my clue to stop sending them."

"I'm sorry you and Sasha didn't work out. I know you cared for both of them deeply." I glanced at Amy, who was being very quiet and had her head down, focused on her plate. Greg, who sat next to me, avoided my gaze when I went to him for support. I guess it was up to me. "But isn't it time to get out there again? Start dating?"

"Jill," Greg warned.

"Greg, leave her be. She's just being honest. Yes, Jill, I need to move on. Sasha has, and she and Olivia will be happy with this new guy. Although I think he looks a little cheesy and fussy from the Facebook posts she's putting up. In that suit he looks like he's never fixed a flat tire or put up new shelves in a room. Definitely not a strong, manly man like me." Toby grinned and put out his arms in a fake muscleman flex. "But she gets to pick who she's seeing, not me. And I'm going to start dating again. Soon. I just haven't been attracted to anyone. Yet."

"I should have known you were okay." I leaned back in my chair, relieved that Toby truly seemed okay about the breakup. He'd been in a dark place when they'd ended it, but now it seemed like he was ready to move on. "When the student is ready an instructor will appear."

"Are you quoting Buddha?" Amy asked.

I shook my head. "Not sure, but I read it in a book last week. The guy had been broken up for years when a girl walked into his life and changed his world. I love romance."

Amy beamed. "Me too. Send me a link to that book. I think I need to read it right now. To reconfirm that romance is alive and well. There wasn't a jilted bride in the story, right?"

"No wedding until the end." I tried to remember the book title. Then I realized I had stacks of the books on my office desk. "Hold on a moment."

I ran into the office, found the book, and came back. I handed it to Amy. "Here you go. Make sure you write a review as soon as it comes out. Free books come with responsibilities."

"I don't really have time..." Amy started, but I hadn't quite let go of the book. She tried to jerk it out of my hand, then sighed. "You're right. I'll write a review."

"The author thanks you." I went back to my seat. As I cleaned my plate, I glanced around the table. "There's pie for dessert."

"Sound amazing." Greg got up and rinsed his plate. He got small plates from the cupboard, then paused, looking directly at Amy. "I'll get out the pie. Everyone's in for some sweets, right?"

"I might as well. I've eaten enough today that one slice of pie won't change the five pounds I'm going to have gained when I get on the scale tomorrow." Amy picked up her empty plate as well as my own. Toby was finishing the last piece of chicken he'd snagged. No matter what he was feeling, his appetite stayed level. Which meant he could eat a lot of food.

"Anyone up for some cards or a game tonight?" Greg glanced around the table. "I'm feeling like I need a distraction from the investigation. And if it's just Jill and me, she'll try to pump me for information."

"Sounds good, but I've got to leave by nine." Toby finished his chicken and took his plate to the sink and handed it to Amy, who was finishing the rinsing.

"Me too. Mayor Baylor wants to finish our quarterly financial report for the Council tomorrow, which means he'll be nitpicking every line item out there." Amy grimaced at the thought. "At least I'll be too busy to think about Justin."

Greg glanced at me and I shook my head. Toby must have picked up on our nonverbals too because he left the comment alone.

"So no Risk. What about some Pictionary?" Toby looked hopefully at the rest of us.

"You and Amy take your pie into the office and pick out a game. Jill and I will clean up and bring our pie with us in just a few minutes." Greg opened the dishwasher and started loading the dirty plates.

"Okay, when did cleaning up become a euphemism for kissing?" Toby teased as he put a slice of pie on each plate.

"Since get your butt out of the kitchen and mind your own business." Greg pointed a fork at Toby. Then he looked at me. "Is this what it's going to be like when we have kids?"

"I don't know, but if it is, maybe we should just raise golden retrievers. The puppies go away after a few months rather than twenty years," I pointed out.

"Unless you get a kid like Deek, who stays on through his master's program," Toby reminded me.

Both Greg and I groaned at the thought.

Amy and Toby left the kitchen, laughing. Greg moved closer to me. "You clean off the table, I'll do the rest of the dishes."

I pulled out a storage bag. "Do you want this chicken or should I offer it to Toby?"

"I thought Amy brought it. Won't she want to take it home?" Greg closed the dishwasher after putting in the other plates. It wasn't full, so he didn't run it.

"She did bring the food. But she won't take any of it home. In fact, I'm surprised she bought it and ate it. That girl's been a health-food nut for years. She eats pretty clean even at the diner. Fried chicken is not on her menu." I stared toward the living room. "She's worried about Justin. I swear, if he stands her up, I'm going to track him down and kill him."

Greg put his hands over his ears. "Why do you say these things while I'm in the room? And no, I don't want the chicken. Send it home with Toby."

"He'll make it last a few more meals, which means his food costs for the week will go down. And that is more money he can put in his dream house fund." I repurposed one of the sacks and put the leftover chicken and sides back inside. Then I put the whole thing in the fridge. I wiped down the table and glanced around the room. It was clean enough. Time to play.

By the time Amy and Toby had left the sun had dropped into the ocean and it was dark. Amy had driven to my house, so she left by herself. Toby, well, he lived in the very nice shed behind my house, so he didn't have far to go. As Greg and I stood on the front porch, I nodded over to Esmeralda's house. A Range Rover sat in the driveway next to Rory's BMW. Lights blazed in the little house. "Looks like they have a party going on."

"That's Nic's SUV. He must still be in town. He told me he had some business in the city, but he'd be back in town this week. I guess that's what happened." Greg put his arms around me. "Your arms are freezing. Let's go inside."

Amy's car had disappeared and Esmeralda's house wasn't telling me any secrets, so I followed Greg inside and we sat in front of the television watching a cooking show until I felt my eyes dropping off.

"Time to crash?" Greg asked.

"What gave me away? My closed eyes?" I yawned and stood up slowly. It was time to go to bed.

He shook his head. "Your snore."

My nightmares were filled with two camps. Those who knew what was going on because they'd staged the play, including the death of Nan Gunter, owner of Grow Rich Today. I sat in the audience and tried to ask questions, but they ignored my raised hand. And when Amy tried to help, saying she'd ask the question for me, the one she actually asked hadn't been the question I needed. Instead, she was asking about Justin and why he was still in Nebraska.

I woke up in the middle of the night in a cold sweat. Emma stood next to me, licking my arm to wake me up. I must have been talking in my sleep. I rubbed her head, then patted the bed next to me, scooting closer to Greg so I could make room for her. She jumped up and cuddled. I kissed her head and whispered, "Do me a favor and chase all the bad dreams away tonight, okay?"

Chapter 16

I woke alone in the bed when my alarm went off. By the time I got downstairs Emma was in her dog bed sleeping and Greg had already left. I picked up the note from the table. I unfolded it and read it aloud: "'Emma's been fed. Don't let her tell you otherwise. I hope to see you tonight but I may be late. Go ahead and eat without me.'"

Emma glanced at me, then at her bowl with a hopeful whine. I shook my head. "Sorry girl, Greg ratted you out."

I made some toast for breakfast and added a banana. I was hoping eating something at home would keep me from grabbing a cookie or two during my shift. Then I poured my walking cup full of coffee and left the house to go open the store.

Aunt Jackie had reviewed my street fair plan with minimal notes and changes. She'd liked almost everything. Which was so unlike her, I almost decided to close the shop and go down to Harrold's train shop to see if she was okay. But it was still early. She might not appreciate my early morning humor or visit.

I started coffee and my commuters started showing up. I enjoyed chatting with them, mostly because I knew they'd be in and out. I'm not much for long conversations with strangers. By the time that rush was over the shop was dead. I ran through the chore list Aunt Jackie left me, then went back to the office to pick out an Advanced Reader Copy to spend the rest of my morning with.

I heard the bell go off right as I was deciding between two books. I took both out with me and Neal Cole was standing at my cash register. On the wrong side of the counter.

He dropped his hands and grinned. "Hey, there you are. I've been waiting out here for a while, so I thought I'd come knock on your office door."

What a liar. Walking over, I stood between him and the register, setting down the books. "Sorry, customers aren't allowed back here. Health department orders."

He held up his hands. "Oops. Sorry. I didn't realize I was breaking the law."

"What can I get you?" I watched as he backed out of the area. The cash register wouldn't work without a key and I had that on a stretchy on my wrist. We typically only had one person on staff at a time, so it was policy to keep the key with us to make sure that no one ran off with the day's profits while we were bringing out more cheesecake.

"Coffee, black." He pulled out a five and glanced at the menu board. "A large to go."

"Coming right up." I wasn't going to confront him about the lie, but at least I knew what kind of man he was now. And sometimes having that information was all you needed to know about someone. "We really had fun at the painting event last week."

He snorted. "Meredith puts on a great party, doesn't she?"

Odd response. I slipped the sleeve on the cup and tightened down the lid. "Too bad about what happened to Nan later. You said you knew them? How well?"

"I didn't say I knew them." He pushed the five closer to me.

I rang up the charge and opened the register. "Actually, you did. You told Greg and me both that you met at the winery. Was that why Nan came back to the studio after everyone left?"

"You ask a lot of questions for a coffee girl." He held out his hand for his change and I laid it and the receipt on his palm.

"I like to know where I stand with people." I smiled. "Tell Meredith I said hi."

He nodded, then hurried out of the shop. He paused and turned back before he hit the door but must have changed his mind about what he was going to say when Deek entered the shop.

Deek nodded toward him, then walked directly to me and threw his bag on the counter. He glanced back at Neal, who stared at the two of us, then barreled out of the front door. "What was that about?"

"I have no idea." I peeked at the schedule. "You're not due here for a couple of hours. Did you come in early to write?"

Deek went around to pour himself a cup of coffee. Then he looked at the door again. "Let's just say I felt like I needed to show up a little early."

"Did you have a vision?" I smiled, teasing him.

He sipped his coffee, staring at me, then at the door. "Do you really want to know?"

Knowing his family history, maybe I didn't. I already didn't like it when Esmeralda got one of her trance messages around me. I didn't need Deek doing the same thing. "No, actually, I don't. Did you bring your laptop to work?"

"Have laptop, will write." He smiled and took the bag and his coffee over to his favorite table. With his back against the wall and a clear view of the entrance, he reminded me of the way Greg chose our tables when we went out for dinner or a drink. He always wanted to be able to watch the entrances.

I chose one of the books and moved over to the couch. Then I watched Deek watch the door for a few minutes before I got bored with the game and started reading. At eleven customers started to come in for a coffee and a treat. I was too busy to read from then to one, when my shift ended. Deek came on at noon, and between the two of us, we handled the semi lunch crowd. The difference between CBM's lunch crowd and Diamond Lille's was that my customers usually came in for a book or two. The coffee and cheesecake seemed like more of an afterthought than a real meal. Or, more likely, a reward for finding the perfect book.

When I got ready to go I thought about boxing up some cookies to take over to the Drunken Artist Studio. I hadn't really welcomed Meredith and Neal to town yet.

"I wouldn't do that. Not today." Deek took the box out of my hand and put it back on the shelf.

"What are you talking about?"

He leaned on the counter. "Look, I know you want to go snooping, but I've got a really bad feeling about that guy today. And it's not going away. I think you should ask your police dude for a ride home."

"You want me to bother Greg in the middle of the investigation?" I shook my head. "I've been walking home for years. Never once did I have a problem."

"I know. It's just …" Deek looked at me, worry filling his face.

I sighed. "You have a bad feeling."

"Yes. Exactly." Deek brightened, pulling out his phone. "If police dude can't take you home, I bet my mom is still in town. She can drive you home. And it won't even be a problem."

I wondered how often Deek had these feelings. "Look, I'm going to go to Diamond Lille's and have lunch. I'll call you when I get home so you won't have to worry."

"Did someone say lunch?" Greg's voice boomed from the front door. I narrowed my eyes at Deek. "Did you call him?"

"Me?" He squeaked. "I don't even have his number."

Greg looked from Deek to me. "Did I step into something?"

"You're telling me that you just happened to come and get me for lunch?" I wasn't sure I believed either of them.

"You don't want to go to lunch?" Greg put the back of his hand on my forehead. "Are you sick?"

I pushed his hand away. "Come on, let's go. Just know you're going to have to walk me home too. Deek's worried about me."

"Wait, what happened? Why am I walking you home? And why is Deek concerned?" Greg followed me out of the coffee shop and down the street. "Jill, hold up. What are you not telling me?"

I glanced around the street. We had a lot of tourists for a Wednesday, but I'd heard the bed-and-breakfasts had been booked solid for the week because of the upcoming festival. Josh and Kyle, his assistant, were working on a pergola for the street fair to allow them to put a sun cover over the antique furniture they were bringing out to the booth. Josh eyed me suspiciously, like I was going to tell him he wasn't allowed to make the temporary shelter.

I wanted to mess with him, act like I'd brought Greg with me for muscle when I told him to tear it down, but I just didn't have the heart to tease him. Not today. Besides, Greg wasn't going to let this walking me home go without an explanation. I smiled and waved at Josh. Kyle waved back. Josh stared at me, shocked at the gesture. Seriously, the man needed to lighten up.

When we were past Antiques by Thomas and the crowd had lightened a little, I took Greg's arm in mine and slowed to a steady stroll. "Look, promise you won't get mad or go talk to the guy and I'll tell you what happened."

"You want me to promise before you tell me? How bad is this?" He didn't stop walking, but I felt his muscles tense under my arm.

"Not bad, just kind of weird. I was in the back and I think Neal Cole thought he could rob my register when he came in for coffee."

Greg's head turned sharply and watched my face for a few steps. "You're not pressing charges? Why?"

"Because his story could have been true? It wasn't, and I know he was at least checking out the till to see how easy it would be. I just came out too quickly for him to realize he wasn't going to be able to do anything without the key." We crossed the road before we were in the middle of the crowd at Austin's Bike Shop.

We resumed our stroll toward lunch. Greg looked down at me. "Maybe he had a gun. If he had a gun, you would have had to give him the key." "He owns a business here. How long is he going to be able to stay in town if he robbed me at gunpoint?" I shook my head. "No, it wasn't planned. He just saw what he thought was an opportunity and he tried it. Which makes me worry more about the fact he owns a business here. He seems a little shifty. Did you do a background check on them when they filed for their business license?"

"No. The studio is solely owned by Meredith. Honestly, I was surprised to find out she was married when they opened. None of her accounts are joint. She owns the building in her name only as well." Greg paused at the end of the parking lot to Diamond Lille's. "So at the time she got her license, Esmeralda only did the one. After the murder I realized our mistake and ordered one on Neal. The PI in Bakerstown isn't as quick as Esmeralda is, so I'm picking it up today."

I nodded toward the diner. "You don't want to talk about this at lunch, do you?"

He put his hand behind my head and pulled me in for a kiss. "You're very perceptive. But I agree with Deek. I'm a little nervous about the guy and his thoughts about you as well. Do me a favor and drive to work the next few days until we can get this cleared up?"

"It was already on my schedule. Except maybe Friday and Saturday. You might have to walk me in. Getting a car in and out of town is going to be a madhouse during the festival." I put my hand on his chest when he started to move. "One more thing: I want to talk to Meredith about Nan and Steve. Maybe she knows something she didn't tell you in your interview."

"I don't want you near Neal." Greg's voice was firm.

"Honestly, *I* don't want to be near Neal. He gives me the creeps." I glanced toward the end of town where my shop sat. "What if I bring Evie with me? That way it could be seen as a way to get Evie more acquainted with other women in the area. A girl-to-girl visit. And I'll bring cookies."

"Remember the time you almost got you and your aunt burned to a crisp by trying to pick up our vacation tickets?" He nodded toward the diner and we started walking.

"Basically, you're saying even my normal life activities tend to put me in danger, so visiting the studio should be fine because we're already suspicious of the occupants. Or at least one of them." I flashed a bright smile as he held the door open for me.

He chuckled. "Not what I said, but you've always followed your own star. Just text me when you go and when you're out of there. If I don't get a text, I'll come find you and embarrass you in front of your friends."

"Now I sound like I have a curfew." I waved to Carrie and pointed to our booth. Instead of the smile and nod, I got a curt nod.

"Wow. What did you do to make Carrie mad? And can I sit somewhere besides with you?"

"Way to be supportive. And it wasn't me; Toby called her 'princess.'" I gently pushed him into the booth and sat on the other side. "Well, and Evie had dinner with Doc. But it was just about the murder. And I thought Carrie was over that. Just don't abandon me."

"Okay. I guess I have to stay with you." He glanced over the menu. "Stuffed meat loaf it is."

"Of course that's what you'd choose; it's Wednesday." I laughed at I put the menu away. "I'm just as bad. I'm having my stress meal: fish and chips with a vanilla shake. It's a good thing stress increases my metabolism."

"You're perfect just the way you are." Greg smiled, and for the millionth time I realized why I'd fallen in love with him.

By the time we'd finished lunch and he'd walked me home, I realized I didn't want to risk running today either. Or at least not until Greg had figured out what was up with our new friend Neal. I grabbed the book I'd been reading and, with a glass of iced tea, took Emma out into the yard to play. She had a system of checking the entire fence line so she could make sure there weren't any roving rabbits in her yard. She loved the process almost as much as running with me.

The light was fading when I finished the book. Toby pulled his truck into the driveway and Emma ran to meet him. He waved and nodded to the gate, his way of asking if he could come visit. Even though he basically lived in my backyard, I hardly ever saw him around. Which was a testament to how much he worked.

"Hey, Jill, how are you?" Toby sat on the steps, leaning against the railing so he could watch me, and started playing ball with Emma.

"Greg told you, huh?" I closed the book and set it on my lap.

"He mentioned it. There's no way anyone's getting into that register without a key. You're not worried about Neal trying again, are you?" Toby threw the ball over the hill in the backyard.

"Maybe a little. Not on my shift. I think he knows I didn't believe his story about why he was behind the counter. But Aunt Jackie? I'd hate it if something happened and we knew he was a problem and didn't do anything." I blurted out the one worry that had been bugging me all day.

"What would my aunt do if she caught Neal trying to steal from us? She wouldn't be so forgiving. And he might overreact."

"Harrold's been coming to work with her for the last week. He sits at the table and works crosswords. Then they go home together after her shift. I figured you knew." Toby shrugged. "Harrold's not much of a bodyguard, but she's never alone in the shop. I think that makes him feel better."

"I'm going to lose my closer soon. I knew when they got married things would change."

Toby shook his head. "I don't think so. Both of them seem to like the situation. It gets them out and around people. Some of Harrold's friends have started coming by at night just to chat. It's kind of nice having an older group hanging around. It used to be a teenage crowd at night. Mostly because your aunt doesn't make them buy something, like Lille does."

I felt blindsided. I didn't realize much about what was happening during my aunt's shifts. I should have known this was happening. "I guess maybe I need to talk to my aunt more."

Toby shook his head. "No, you don't. The two of you were close before she was married. Now she and Harrold are figuring out these things together. She doesn't need you hovering."

"You're saying the bird has left the nest?" I chuckled as I realized he was right. My aunt and her new husband needed to figure out things on their own. I didn't have to fix everything.

"I'm saying you're not in charge of everything that happens to those around you. Even when you're just trying to be kind." He wiped his hand on the deck after Emma brought him a very soggy ball to throw.

My phone rang. Looking at the display, I held it up. "Do I tell my boyfriend I'm sitting on the porch with a cute guy?"

"If you want me to continue to be healthy enough to pay rent, I'd say no." He stood and brushed off his pants. "I'm heading in to eat, then crash. It's been a long week."

I answered as I watched him cross over to the gate that led to his shed-slash-apartment. "Hey, Greg. Toby says hi."

"Where are you? Home? Good." He paused. "I was going to tell Toby this as well, so this saves me time."

Hearing the stress in his voice, I picked up my book and Emma and I went inside. I sat down at the table after locking the back door. "Actually, he just left to make some dinner, then he's crashing. What's going on?"

"Your friend Neal has a criminal record. That's why she doesn't have him on any of the financial documents. The last stint he did time for was some sort of Ponzi scheme. Money laundering, embezzlement—this guy has problems with money. I've got a friend over at the city records department who's pulling his old rap sheet. It's all white collar and he's got more than one conviction."

I'd been afraid of that. The guy had just seemed too polished when I'd caught him with his hand almost in the proverbial cookie jar. He lied like he'd had a lot of practice. "Any violent crimes in his background?"

"Not sure yet. That's why I have my friend pulling his actual sheet. I have a feeling he's good at making charges go away."

I thought about Nan and her condition on the night she'd been murdered. Maybe Neal had been trying his tricks on a new mark and she'd caught on?

I pulled my sweater closer as I said goodbye to Greg after promising to stay inside with the doors locked. South Cove felt a little less safe right now after one phone call. And that made me mad.

Chapter 17

My shift on Thursday went by too quickly. Some days were like that. Others dragged on like they were years long instead of just twenty-four hours. The store was busy with customers and we were all pushing to be ready for Friday's start of the St. Patrick's Day festival. I still had to run to Bakerstown, which made my driving into work at least a little less unnecessary. But I was making Greg happy, so there was that as well. I just hated changing my life because someone else was being stupid.

Deek glanced at the to-do list as I checked off my shopping list. "Is Sadie coming in to stock today? I looked in the walk-in and we're short on desserts."

"I think so. I'll give her a call when I get in the car just to make sure, though. Usually she does her deliveries early, so I should have seen her during my shift." Now I had one more thing to be worried about. "Who did the order last week?"

"Your aunt. She said she wanted to make sure we were well-stocked for the street fair." Deek nodded to the door. "I guess you don't have to call now."

Sadie Michaels's little purple PT Cruiser pulled up in front of the shop. I watched as my friend got out and opened the back. I nodded to Deek. "Go help her get everything in. I'll stay and watch the register."

I didn't mean it literally, but after yesterday maybe I should be more focused on making sure things were secure. I took the clipboard Deek had been using and started checking off items and making sure my shopping list was complete.

Deek and Sadie came inside. He held a large box, but Sadie's arms were empty. "Do you need me to help carry in the rest?"

"That's all of it. Your aunt said a normal order when I called Friday night to check." She shook her head, watching my face react. "You were expecting more. I knew it. With the street fair, Lille tripled her orders and even the Castle doubled what they typically order. I should have called you to double-check, but you know Jackie. She gets grumpy if you don't do what she says."

"I'm so sorry. I don't know what she was thinking." I motioned for Deek to put the box on the counter and checked what was inside. It might keep us in treats for Friday. But Saturday we'd be out of everything when we opened the doors. "I hate to ask, but can you get us three times this?"

Sadie pulled out her phone and scrolled through something. I assumed she was checking her orders. "Look, I'm baking tomorrow for Lille's Saturday treats. I can add you in there. I'd bake today, but Bill and I have tickets for a concert in the city tonight. I don't know if I can get you all of what you need, but if you don't care what I make, or that I won't be able to deliver until late Friday, I should be able to keep you kind of stocked."

"Sadie, I owe you big-time. Whatever you can bring us." I nodded to Deek, who took the box back into the office to unpack and put the cheesecakes in the walk-in. I waited for him to leave, then leaned close to Sadie, hoping Deek wouldn't overhear. "I can't believe Aunt Jackie messed up this order so bad."

"Maybe she was just busy and didn't think about the fair being this weekend," Sadie offered as an explanation. "Don't overthink this. Talk to her and let her know what happened. Then let her tell her story. Knowing you, you're probably already at brain tumor as the most likely cause."

"It's not totally out of the range of possibility." I hated that my friend knew me so well. I had been thinking seizure, but she'd nailed my concern about a serious health condition causing her forgetfulness. "You're right. I need to just point out the error and ask what the heck she was thinking. Man, that's going to go over well."

"Better you than me." Sadie patted my hand and smiled. "I've got to go grab some shut-eye. I'll see you tomorrow."

I watched as my friend left the shop. A few years ago she would have dropped heaven and hell to help me, but a year ago she was a widowed mom raising a great kid who had gone away to college and made a life for himself. A really good life. Sadie and her son, Nick, were good people. I just needed to realize I was going to run short on food this weekend. Unless there was a really bad rainstorm that kept everyone home.

A girl could hope.

I decided running to Bakerstown would give me time to stop at the local bakery there to see what I could get from them to fill in the missing spots. And I didn't have time to do that and stop at the Drunken Artist to try to chat with Meredith. I'd just have to find time for her after the festival was over.

I dialed Aunt Jackie's number as I drove to Bakerstown. When she answered I decided the roundabout method was probably going to be the easiest. "Hey, do you need anything in town? I'm running to grab decorations and more bakery items."

"What do you mean, more bakery items? Didn't Sadie deliver today?"

So much for subtle. I just should have said I was going into town. "She did, but she said she didn't get an extra food order for the festival. I guess you didn't realize it was this weekend?"

"Seriously? You think I messed up the order? I sent her an email detailing everything we wanted. I bet we won't be able to get the mint-green cheesecakes now. That's a shame."

"Wait, you sent her an email? Sadie said she had to call you." Now I was totally confused.

"I sent her an email Thursday night while Harrold watched the store. I wrote a note in the festival plan, listing out what I'd ordered and when. Sadie called to verify the order I'd placed and I told her yes, that was what we needed."

I sighed. Sadie had been talking about the regular order. My aunt had been talking about the order from the email. Lines had gotten crossed, and like most errors in everyday life, no one was really to blame. And I'd jumped to the conclusion that my aunt was losing her marbles. I filed away this conversation for later and hoped I wouldn't make the same mistake again. But I probably would. I cared for my aunt, and for the last year or so she'd been scaring me. Too vulnerable, making poor choices, and now she was married and not even asking my advice anymore.

"Look, I'm near the store. Is there anything specific you need from town?"

"Not really. Just play up the green. And special. I know we'll have to pay more to get anything at this late date, but mistakes happen." She laughed, and I realized she was also talking to Harrold. "I've got to go, dear. Harrold and I are making dinner so we don't have to eat after my shift."

I tucked my phone back into a cubby in the car and turned up the music. I had a way to go to get to Bakerstown and all I wanted to do right now was listen to some music and not think about the ways my life was changing.

I stopped at the party store first. I wandered through the store and picked up a few extra items, including a large, prewrapped box to put some things inside. Having Olivia's birthday present checked off my list would be a big relief. I'd take the box and St. Patrick's Day goodies and leave it in my car. Then I could stuff it with books and toys from the store before closing it up for Evie to take to the party.

I missed Sasha. One more change in my life that I hadn't gotten over totally. She'd been a fun addition to the CBM staff. And her daughter, Olivia, had been our kid mascot for the years that Sasha had been part of our family.

I headed to the customer service station and realized I was standing behind Meredith. Sometimes I was just in the right place at the right time. "I take it you're buying decorations for this weekend too? I swear I'm going to be more organized next year. I know I have a ton of green beads somewhere in storage."

Meredith turned my way and I saw the bruise on her cheek as she lifted her hand to her face to try to hide it. "Oh, Jill, I'm sorry, I didn't realize it was you."

"Oh my God, Meredith, what happened?" I tried to look around her fingers. She had what my aunt would have called a whale of a shiner.

She waved her hand around it dismissively. "You'll never believe me. I rolled over in the middle of the night and fell out of bed. But on the way down my cheek found my nightstand. I'm lucky I didn't break a bone."

I didn't really think the bruise looked like it came from a nightstand. It looked more like a fist. A big, male fist. But I decided to play along. Maybe I could actually get something out of her if I did. "That's awful. But it sounds like something I'd do. Greg is always saying I'm a klutz. He worries that people will think he's hitting me or something. People can be so cruel and nosy."

"That's so true." She glanced at the clerk. There were two people still in front of her. She couldn't escape yet. "So, are you looking forward to the festival?"

"I love our community events. Darla does such a good job and she's so creative. You're going to love being part of the South Cove business group. We're like one big family. Always there for one another."

That got me a wince from Meredith. Which had been my aim. Either she was going to talk to me or she'd pack up in the middle of the night to get away from the town's prying eyes.

"Well, I'm more of a private person. Hopefully there's room for all types." Meredith glanced over at the woman in front of her. She had just started digging for her receipts for what looked like several returns. I saw her judge the wait time versus just leaving and dealing with what she had.

Apparently she didn't have much in the way of decorations because she firmed her bottom lip and moved up a few inches to stay.

"Of course there is. I'm private too." I lowered my voice into a whisper. "I felt so bad about what happened to Nan. How in the world did she get back in your shop?"

Her eyes widened and she shook her head. "I'm not sure. I guess she broke in. Or I didn't engage the lock like I should have. When I went down the next morning and found her, I couldn't believe she was dead. She looked so peaceful."

"How well did you know her?"

Meredith shrugged. "Not at all. I had only met her that night, when she and her husband Terry came in for the class."

"Steve. His name is Steve." Now I knew she was playing some kind of game. She at least knew the name of the man whose wife had been killed in her shop.

She held up a finger and grinned when a new clerk showed up to help with the line. "That's right. Steve. Anyway, it was nice seeing you."

"You too."

I watched as she moved to the counter. She'd totally dismissed me. She smiled at the clerk. "Good afternoon, I'm next. You have an order waiting for Meredith Cole?"

I rewound my encounter with Meredith several times as I stood in line at the bakery, my last stop. It had been weird, and it wasn't just my interpretation of the chat. When it was my turn a bubbly twenty-year-old behind the counter greeted me with an open box.

"Good afternoon. I'm Chrissy. What can I box up for you?" She held out a set of tongs in her gloved hand.

"Hi, Chrissy. I'm Jill Gardner from Coffee, Books, and More in South Cove. I was wondering if you had a manager here I could talk to about a bulk purchase?"

Chrissy looked confused but set down the box and tongs. "Hold on a second. I'll run in the back to see if Megan can talk with you. Jill from Coffee, Books, and More, right?"

"That's my name. I'll be over here at the side of the counter." I smiled and turned to the person in line behind me. "Sorry for the delay."

He didn't even look up from his phone. "No problem. This place is always slow."

I stepped over to the side and let him approach the counter, where the overbubbly Chrissy would be right back to take his order. It took her a little longer than anyone had expected, and I saw a few puzzled looks thrown my way, like I'd made the bakery staff disappear.

Finally Chrissy came back. She didn't look my way as she picked up the box, but she spoke to me before greeting the next customer. "She'll be right out."

Five minutes and two more customers served and out of the building, a frazzled-looking woman hurried out of the back. Her hair was pulled up into a messy bun and she held a notepad. Her gaze swept the room, then fell on me. "Sorry. Chrissy should have asked you to sit and offered you some coffee."

"I'm fine, but should we sit?" I pointed to the closest table.

She nodded, but paused by Chrissy. "Bring us out a plate of assorted cookies and two coffees. Black?"

When I nodded she grinned. "I knew you were my kind of people. I think you'll like our blend. I've been to your shop before and your coffee is top-notch too."

We settled at a table and she held out her hand. "Megan Miracle. Yes, that's my real name. So of course I open a small-town bakery. There's no way I could have been a lawyer or a doctor with that last name."

I laughed and realized I agreed with her. We were the same type of person. Friendly, personable, and willing to laugh at ourselves. Chrissy quickly delivered the cookies and coffee and just as quickly disappeared back behind the counter.

Megan watched her hurry back to the next customer. "The girl is outgoing, but she doesn't think ahead. Too bad. I was hoping for a leader in this hire."

"Getting the right hire is sometimes a chore." I knew how hard it could be to find the right fit for our team. And we didn't have a production line in the back of the shop like a bakery did. "Anyway, I need a favor. The store messed up on our desserts order for this weekend and I was wondering if you had anything you could sell us. I could come tomorrow morning to pick it up if need be."

"Green frosted cupcakes, cookies, that kind of thing? We don't do cheesecake here." Megan laughed at my shocked face. "I told you I've been to your store. I'd love to have a more permanent relationship, but I know you have a connection with Pies on the Fly."

"Sadie and I are friends, but I probably could increase my inventory. Cupcakes and cookies would be perfect. Let's hammer out the details for this weekend, then I'll get with my aunt and we'll figure out a starting weekly delivery amount." I listed off what I'd need, and as she made notes and quoted a price, something caught my eye outside the window. I frowned and then walked over to the window. I hadn't realized exactly where the bakery was located. I was a block away from the abandoned building site for Steve's company.

I pointed to the farmhouse sitting down the road. "Do you know anything about that plot of land?"

"The old Mason house? It was supposed to be under development for a business commercial property a couple of years ago. I'd thought about buying the place next door and opening a joint café there. I'm so glad I didn't." Megan handed me my copy of the order and pointed to a house next door that currently held a real estate office. "Here you go. I'll go box up what we have on hand and have the rest delivered tomorrow morning. Six okay?"

"That will work. Thanks." I tucked the order into my tote. "Can I ask you a question?"

"About the delivery?"

I shook my head. "No, about why you didn't expand. With a large commercial building down the street a café would have brought in a lot of money, especially when there's nothing like it nearby. Why did you just stay with the bakery?"

She stared out at the abandoned farmhouse, not, as I had expected, at the cute house-turned-office next door. "There was just something about the deal that bothered me. I've lived in the area all my life. There were rumors even before the Mason house was abandoned that it was haunted. They had a kid; older than me, but I'd seen him around. He just looked shell-shocked most of the time. I just didn't trust that the deal would go through. Believe me, tearing down that place and the barn behind it would do a lot to increase property values. I just didn't think the house would go easy."

"I get that feeling from it as well." I stared at the house with her. "Hey, what was the kid's name who lived there? Do you remember?"

"I can't forget it. His name was Steve. And they thought he murdered his parents."

Chapter 18

One of the crazy things these days is that every town has its haunted house story. In South Cove it was the witch's house that had been torn down for condos a year ago. Bakerstown apparently had two. The old funeral home, Bakerstown Memorial, had been suspected of burning bodies for a serial killer. And the Mason house.

I scrolled through the website, focusing on haunted sites on the California coast. I'd dropped off the pastries at Coffee, Books, and More and had come straight home to start researching. And what I'd found out was that our little slice of heaven was known for some pretty scary history. And if you dropped into Los Angeles, you could add a lot more hauntings to the list.

And someone loved to do history on the sites. I read through the Mason house history. The family had been wealthy, and one of the large farms in the area had sold off land for the origins of Bakerstown. But instead of taking that money and rebuilding the farmhouse, the patriarch had just put the money in the bank. Which he lost most of during the depression of 1920, proving the warning about putting all your eggs in one basket. After that things went downhill for the Masons. The oldest boy kept trying to work the farm, his brothers and sisters leaving for better jobs anywhere else. Then the parents died within two months of each other and it was just the son, his wife, and their boy, Stephen. The new owner of the farm didn't survive much past his parents' death dates, when he was caught in a baler accident. The website didn't say, but insinuated it was a bloody and gruesome death. Mrs. Mason and then five-year-old Stephen left town and the farm fell into disrepair. Soon ghost sightings were starting to be reported and the legend was born.

Could Steve Gunter be Stephen Mason? Did his mother remarry?

I wrote down all my questions. If this was true, Steve really was having a cursed life. Losing his grandparents, then his dad, then his own son, and finally his wife? I thought that could drive anyone insane, which could explain his actions over at Esmeralda's. I wondered how much of this Greg knew.

Esmeralda would say it was the ghosts in a period of unrest that provoked Steve's actions. I thought a more likely explanation was the guy made his own crazy. Either way I was starting to question Steve's sanity. I glanced at my watch. Greg still wasn't home and I had a busy day ahead of me with the start of the St. Patrick's Street Fair tomorrow. I closed down the laptop after sending Greg the link for the haunted house site. Then I cleared up the house and went to bed.

The next morning, after checking on the delivery from Miracle Bakery, I searched through our local charm books to see if there was anything about the Mason house. I found three different books had it listed and I copied the pages for Greg. He'd been gone when I'd woke up; in fact, I wasn't sure he'd even came home. I'd say it was a good sign that maybe the investigation had broken, but I thought it was more likely he'd had to do both the investigation and get ready for this weekend's festival. Maybe I'd pop over when Deek got here and deliver a coffee care package along with the pages about the house.

Deek arrived at nine and we set up the outside booth for the festival. I'd stay on and work his shift inside until Evie came on. Then Deek would tag team with her until Jackie showed up this evening. Tomorrow we'd start the day with two people on duty and then rotate through the day. Without Toby, we really needed one more person on staff. But with him, which was most of the time, we were fully staffed. I needed to see what I could do about hiring someone just for the festival times. I tucked a strand of hair behind my ear and put that worry off to another day. Today was all about the festival and not getting behind. And making sure Evie had some room for her kid corner duties.

After we finished the set up I glanced at the clock. The crowd hadn't arrived yet. I poured a carafe of coffee and boxed up some cookies. "I'll be right back."

"Tell police dude hi."

Deek was scary good at guessing my intention. I *had* been going to see Greg, but I could just as well have been going to the Drunken Artist Studio to drop off a welcome gift. I nodded and took off before we got busy.

No one was out at the Drunken Artist Studio table. There was a painting of a leprechaun on the table as well as some glitter and some handouts about the events coming up, but neither Neal nor Meredith sat at the table. I waited to cross the street until I'd gotten past the businesses. Which meant I had to walk past Josh. Devil you knew, I guess. I lucked out, and Kyle was outside, arranging a small seating area. "Good morning, Kyle."

"Miss Gardner." He tipped his head. "Great day to be outside selling, right?"

"It's not raining." I grinned. "We should have a lovely weekend."

"Hopefully." He ducked back into the shop to bring out something else.

When I got to the police station Amy had her City Hall table out and she waved to me. "Refreshments?"

"I'm sure Greg won't mind." I crossed the lawn and opened the cookie box. "Coffee?"

"No, I've got a few water bottles on hand. And if I need to, I'll pop inside to refill." Amy took a cookie. "Thanks for bringing me down off the ledge."

"Have you heard from him?" I closed the box.

"A couple of texts saying not to worry. But not a call. Yet. He's going to owe me big for scaring me like this." Amy smiled. "Maybe it's a test of my patience."

"I doubt it. Justin isn't like that."

A couple wandered up to the table and picked up a flyer. The man waved at Amy. "Miss? Can we ask you about real estate here?"

"I'll be right over." She finished the cookie. "Duty calls."

I would need to be quick too. Deek was about to be busy inside and out and he could only deal with one area at a time.

Greg was in the office with Toby and Tim. A few other guys wearing black pants and security T-shirts were in the meeting room. I chose the office. Without knocking, I went inside. "Here's coffee and cookies. I don't think I have enough for the rest of your guys, so don't tell them."

"Thanks, Jill." Greg leaned over and kissed me. "We're a little busy here."

"And I need to run anyway. Stay safe, guys." I turned and hurried out of the police station and back to the shop. I didn't even look at the Drunken Artist Studio or Antiques by Thomas. I was on a mission. Only one person stood at the table where Deek stood talking, but there were several lined up for coffee inside.

The first person in line glanced at me when I came through the door. "Do we order coffee here or out at the table?"

"Here's fine. I had to run a quick delivery." I washed my hands and put on an apron. "What can I get for you?"

By the time it slowed down enough for me to sit down at the counter it was already almost five. We'd underestimated the amount of people who were coming in from the area. It was a madhouse, and with Evie working the kids table, we needed someone at the inside register full-time.

My aunt glanced around the dwindling crowd. "You go home. I'll have Deek clear the outdoor booth and then send him home as soon as Evie clears that last group of kids. Then she and I can finish up."

"Should I call someone in for tomorrow to help?" Saturdays were the big day at these events. Friday was just a warm-up.

"Let's hire someone for Evie to use at the kids table. She can explain what to do, then watch the front counter too. You can go back and forth from inside to out. And I'll come in with Harrold an hour, no, two hours early." She rubbed the back of her neck. "But once this is done we need to talk about hiring someone to cover my shift full-time. I'll play manager rather than work the evening shift. That way we don't affect everyone's hours just to have festival help."

I stared at her. "You must have read my mind. I was thinking the same thing this morning. Well, not about you giving up your shift, but about needing more help."

"It's not rocket science, Jill. South Cove is growing, and we need to expand our capacity to serve the community." She patted my cheek. "Go home. I'll take it from here."

If every part of my body didn't hurt, I would have argued with her. Greg was sitting at one of the tables near the booth, talking with Deek, when I walked outside. "There's my girl. Ready to go grab food together? I won't call it dinner because I haven't eaten since I inhaled two of the cookies you dropped off. And from talking to Deek here, I'm suspecting you haven't either."

I sank into a chair next to him. Glancing around the still-busy street. "You're not wrong. I should have eaten something before I left the house. I'll remember that tomorrow. I think it's going to be even busier."

He grunted. "I've got Toby and Tim off for a few hours to eat and sleep. Then they'll come back and lead the security guys. I'm off until tomorrow morning, but you know that can change with a moment's notice."

I stood and held out my hand. "Then we'd better get moving if you're going to have any real meal today at all. Lille's is doing a corned beef and cabbage special, but I hear Tiny also has pot roast going tonight, with mashed potatoes."

"You had me at pot roast." Greg groaned and stood. He moved me to the side as Candice Frey walked past us and into the store.

I was waiting for the door to close, then pointed at the woman. "That's Steve's mistress. I can't believe she's still walking around. Don't you think she's at least part of the murder plot?"

Greg closed his eyes and groaned. "Sorry, I thought I told you."

"Told me what?" I kept my gaze on Candice as she went directly to the romance shelves.

"One, that I'm the police detective and your job is to sell coffee and books."

I turned to watch Greg staring at me. Deek snickered, and I threw him a glare too. "What's the second thing?"

"She's Steve's sister. Not his mistress. She's his half-sister and the attorney for him and his company. I don't think she killed her sister-in-law. Especially because she didn't get back from New York until the evening after Nan was killed." He blinked his eyes and shrugged. "That's what a real investigator does. He rules out suspects by seeing exactly where they were at the time of the murder. Candice was a conference headliner in a legal convention and she'd just finished a dinner with several of the highest-ranked estate lawyers in the country. She's considered an expert in the legal area."

"She's his sister?" I thought about the scene I'd watched while at dinner the other night. Had it just been a sister comforting her older brother? I wanted to scream. She had been at the top of my suspect pool. Mostly because I felt like she was hiding something. Because she was. She was hiding the fact she was Steve's sister. Now I felt like a fool.

"Yep. So can we go eat? Or do you want me to arrest someone else who didn't have a hand in Nan Gunter's murder?"

He just stood there, waiting for my answer. Candice was still going through the shelves. Looking at her face now, I could see the resemblance even through the window glass. "You must be hungry; you're grumpy."

He paused a minute, then chuckled and took my arm. "I love you, Jill Gardner. Yes, I am hungry. Sorry about snapping at you."

"And in front of my staff." I put the back of my hand on my forehead. "How will I ever recover their respect?"

Now Deek was laughing too. He called after us, "See you in the morning."

I just waved and kept going. Josh and Kyle were busy talking to shoppers as we walked by and I glanced over at the Drunken Art Studio. Meredith was handing out a flyer to someone, but her gaze was on us. When she saw me notice she turned away and started chatting to the person in front of her.

"That's weird," I muttered as we strolled through the dwindling crowd.

Greg's gaze scanned the area around us. "I don't see anything. What are you talking about?"

I kept my gaze forward and pointed toward Austin's Bike Shop. "Don't look back, but Meredith was watching us."

"Are you sure? When I looked over there she was talking to a tourist." He didn't look back, but I felt his body tense beside me.

"Positive. Maybe Neal told her about his slip and she's worried I'm going to tell you." I shook my head. "I don't know how she stays married to him. From what I see, he's kind of a screwup."

"But she loves him," Greg said with a sarcastic laugh. "Maybe people should start thinking about who they fall in love with before the emotion takes over their brain."

"Like you and me." I poked him. "You were on the fence about us for a long time."

He squeezed me. "Not true. I fell in love with you as soon as I was sure you hadn't killed Miss Emily for her money and after your background check came back clean."

"Maybe that's the new dating matchup. You sign up and the system runs a credit and background check on you. Then your potential suitors can check out your stats before seeing if the two of you have chemistry." I pointed to Diamond Lille's. The street had been closed for the weekend, so Lille had set up picnic tables outside in her parking lot. "That's fun."

"It's smart. It doubles her customer space. Do you want to eat inside or out?"

We crossed the street as I considered our options. The weather was spot-on perfect. We had about an hour before the sun set and the town's streetlights would turn on. "Let's eat out here. That way we can enjoy the festival too."

"Sounds great." Greg steered me toward a table on the edge where he could watch the street along with the diners. We passed by Tim and Toby, who were sharing a table and already destroying a couple of Tiny's three-patty hamburgers. We waved but didn't stop. The guys needed their downtime, and besides, they both were eating like they'd missed their last thirty meals.

We settled into a table and a young waitress came by and filled our water glasses and gave us silverware and a menu. Her name tag said Ariel, and I knew I hadn't met her before. But Lille went through servers like a glass of water poured into a strainer. I was surprised that Tiny and Carrie had stayed with her so long. As a boss, Lille was known to be harsh and demanding. I left that to my aunt. I was a good boss; she was the disciplinarian.

"Did I tell you that Aunt Jackie's talking about stepping out of shift work and just doing the management side of the business?" I asked Greg after we'd put in our orders. He'd gotten the pot roast, but I'd gone with a grilled fish dinner with veggies and a side salad. Amy's wedding *was* next weekend.

"It's about time. I've been meaning to talk to you about changing her shift. When she lived in the apartment upstairs it wasn't bad. She didn't have to walk anywhere outside to get home. Now I 'm not sure I'm comfortable with her walking all the way to Harrold's after dark." He checked a text on his phone, answered it, and then put it back away in the carrier.

"Were you going to be the one to tell her she was too old to work the close shift?" I sipped my iced tea and leaned back in the chair, enjoying the quiet. "Because there is no way I am going to do that."

"I know, Jackie can be stubborn. I'd like to think South Cove is safe, but we've had problems with mountain lions lately. And we're too close to the highway. It worries me." He played with his fork as he talked.

"Harrold comes with her now." I smiled as I thought about it. "He's taking this marriage thing seriously. I don't think they've been separated for long since the wedding."

"Harrold isn't going to be able to fight off a mountain lion."

I waved away the concern. "They are driving the few blocks as well. Maybe not tonight because of the festival, but I get your concern. I'm going to start looking for a new hire on Monday. I need someone on staff for when you steal Toby for these festival events."

As if I'd conjured him, Toby stood in front of the table. He didn't look at me; instead, he focused his attention to Greg. My heart sank. Dinner was over before it started. "Boss, we have a problem."

Chapter 19

Greg motioned over our waitress with the plates she was trying to deliver. Toby moved back so she could set down the food. Then she scurried away. Greg picked up his fork and started eating. He nodded to Toby. "Go on, tell me why I'm not going to be able to finish my one meal of the day."

"Sorry, boss. I lost the toss." Toby glanced over to Tim, who had his head down over his plate and seemed to be eating as fast as Greg. "Anyway, we've got a problem over at the Drunken Artist Studio. Steve Gunter is there and causing a scene."

"Are you kidding me? I should have kept him in that jail cell. What does the guy want now?" Greg rolled his eyes. "I swear, I get his grief, but if he doesn't stop causing problems, I'm going to throw him back in a cell just so I know where he is."

Toby shrugged. "Might not be a bad idea, at least until the festival is over. Josh has called three times about this guy yelling at Neal and making the area feel unsafe for customers."

That caught my attention. "Wait, Josh called? Not Meredith or Neal?"

Toby nodded. "The temp we have in Esmeralda's chair says he just keeps calling."

"I know, but if it's that bad, why isn't one of the Coles calling?" I met Greg's gaze. "Unless they don't want anyone to know what Steve's saying."

"Go tell your buddy that as soon as he's done eating, he needs to run over to the Drunken Artist. Let's see what's going on."

Toby turned, then paused. "What about me?"

"Finish your meal, then join him." Greg watched as Toby ran back to the table. "There should be some reward for having to tell the boss his dinner is being interrupted."

"Are you going now?" I eyed his plate. The beef looked tender and smelled amazing. If he had to leave, I could probably snag some of his dinner too. I smiled a bit too brightly and said, "I can have that packaged up and take it home."

"Where you'll eat it. No thanks for the help. I'll finish my meal, then go figure out what's happening at that art shop. I swear, they've been more trouble since they opened than a biker bar on the highway." He pointed to my dinner. "How are the veggies?"

"Fine. Not mashed potatoes, but fine." I speared a piece of broccoli and ate it. I was tired. And if I didn't get home to crash soon, I was going to be grumpy. "Today's one of those days I wish I had a hot tub at the house."

"Your feet hurt?"

I nodded. "My feet, my calves, my hips, my arms, my shoulders." I stretched out my neck just to make sure, then added, "Yep, my neck too. You wouldn't think running a bookstore would be this hard work."

"Which means you had a strong day. Typically you just hang around during your shift looking like a bookstore owner."

"Really? We're talking about who works harder?" It was a game I couldn't win. When I had free time I read. When Greg had free time he went to the gym in the rec hall and worked out. "Let's talk about who killed Nan instead. Since you debunked my top suspect just because she was the victim's sister-in-law, who's on the top of your list?"

He finished his mashed potatoes and took the last bite of his pot roast. I've mentioned Greg belongs to the Clean Plate Club before, haven't I? His phone rang just as he set down the fork. He grinned at me. "Sorry, I need to take this."

"It's probably a spam number and you're just trying to get out of talking to me about this." I called after him as he stepped away from me to take the call. A few diners glanced over our way, and I just smiled and waved. That action could get you out of all kinds of rudeness.

I focused on finishing my fine meal. Not superamazing like a fried fish platter with shrimp and fries, but not bad. I had just finished my salad when Greg came back to the table. He didn't sit down. Instead, he threw two twenties on the table. "That should cover it. I've got to go. Neal's freaking out."

"What do you mean, freaking out?" Concern for Meredith filled my mind.

"He and Steve are both accusing each other of killing Nan. Loudly and in the middle of the St. Patrick's Day festival. Man, I love drinking holidays." He leaned down and kissed me. "I'll see you at home. I don't know how late I'll be, but I'll walk you to the shop."

"Okay then. See you later."

He paused and glanced at me. "Crap, I was supposed to walk you home too."

"I can walk home by myself. You got me most of the way." I sipped my tea. He shook his head, looking around the dining area. "I guess it can't be helped. Come on, Jill, we've got to go now."

I stood. "Look, I can walk home, no problem. It's less than a half mile." He nodded. "Which means I can get there and back quick enough. Look, this isn't a discussion."

"But you were protecting me from Neal. You know exactly where he is and you have two of South Cove's finest with him." I touched his chest. "I'll be fine."

"Okay, so logic isn't an argument I'd thought about." He kissed me. "Okay then, just text me when you're in the house. And please, don't go running."

"Seriously, I have no energy to even walk the beach, let alone run." I sat back down. I was finishing my iced tea and waiting for the waitress to bring back Greg's change. "I'll see you in the morning."

He rubbed his face and nodded. "Just be safe."

"Got it." I watched him stroll out of the parking lot and turn the dining area, and our waitress came over with our check.

"Sorry you had to wait. I've got tables inside as well as you guys." She waited for me to put the money in the folder, then nodded. "I'll be right back with your change."

I took the few minutes to think about what I knew about Meredith and Neal. From what I'd learned lately the woman must be a saint, living with the guy who was always looking for the scam.

When I got home I texted Greg. Safe and sound. Then I found the notebook I'd been using to make notes about Nan's murder. I crossed off Candice. She'd been the perfect suspect in my mind. Well, she had been when I thought she was Steve's mistress. Now that I knew she was his sister, that was a little creepy. I made notes about the land and what my new bakery supplier had told me. Could it be about the land? That had happened before. To me, in fact. Someone had wanted Miss Emily's house as part of a land deal that would have made the developer millions. Maybe this commercial building property was the same way.

I picked up my planner to make a note to go check the filings about the property. Who owned it? Had there been any rezoning requests? Did anything look off? Of course it was Friday after six p.m. The courthouse wouldn't open until Monday. I listed it as one of my must-dos for Monday and closed the calendar. I went back to the notebook and, on a separate sheet, wrote Neal's name. I gave a brief description about the cash register incident and also put a note in about the police event with Steve. Maybe he'd found something that led him to that conclusion. Maybe Steve was just crazy. I closed the notebook and went to veg on the couch with Emma.

* * * *

When I awoke the next morning I was still in my clothes, but instead of being on the couch, I was tucked in bed. I turned off my alarm and stretched as I climbed out. Yesterday had been a workout. Maybe instead of just running all the time I needed to take a weight-lifting class or yoga. Amy was always trying to get me to join her yoga class at the rec hall. The way every muscle in my body ached this morning, I was beginning to think it wasn't a bad idea.

After a shower I felt better and put away the idea of yoga. Again. I hurried downstairs, intent on getting at least a serving of yogurt and a banana in me before I headed to the store and the festival.

There was a basket of oranges, limes, strawberries, apples, and bananas on the table. Greg sat nearby, reading something on his tablet and drinking coffee. He was already dressed and ready for work. He glanced up as I walked in. "Good morning, sunshine. I walked down to the farm stand and got us some fruit and veggies. I put some away in the crisper."

I glanced at the cat clock on the wall that I'd found in an upstairs closet. "It's not even six and they were open?"

"Actually, Mandy was setting up. She likes me, so she let me shop early. Besides, it's always good to be on the right side of the law." He grinned. "And she wanted to talk about Josh. She's thinking he's going to pop the question."

"What question?" I took a single-serve carton of yogurt out of the fridge and found a spoon, then peeled off a banana from the pile. There was no way we were going to eat this much fruit. Unless he thought the fruit would replace my sweet tooth. I narrowed my eyes at him, then looked reflexively at my stomach. Maybe he was trying to tell me something.

"Don't get freaked out. I just wanted some fresh produce and went a little overboard. She has great stuff." He closed his tablet, then refilled his coffee, tucking a couple of apples along with it into his backpack. "And to answer your question, she thinks Josh is going to propose."

I almost choked on my yogurt. "Seriously? I didn't realize they were at that spot. I mean, who in their right mind would date Josh, let alone marry him?"

"Besides your aunt, you mean." A twinkle sparkled in Greg's eye and I knew he was teasing me.

"Okay fine, so he's someone's type. Just not mine. And he's not bad-looking, I guess. Especially now that he's not wearing funeral suits all the time." I finished my yogurt and started on the banana. I could get used to eating before I went to work. Especially if Greg was hanging out with me. We were all domestic right now. It was sweet. "But seriously, it's still Josh."

"If you're coming with me, you'd better get a move on. I need to finish my report on the disturbance at the Drunken Artist Studio." He looked thoughtful. "Maybe it's the name of the studio that causes the disturbances. They've created a wake in the peace zone that is South Cove."

"I'd think it was the bathroom doors. Did you see them? Whoever thought that was real art is completely mental." I stood and threw away my trash, then poured coffee into my travel mug. I topped it off with the last of the coffee from my cup. "All I can say is I'll try to eat some of this before it goes bad."

"Just don't bring home any cheesecake or cookies from the shop tonight. If it doesn't look like the pile is going down, I'll take some to the station." He refilled his coffee. "Are you ready?"

I ran upstairs to grab a light jacket to throw over my capris and some flip-flops to wear once I got to the shop. I slipped on my walking shoes and tucked the flip-flops inside my tote. I checked my hair, then slathered on some sunscreen with a bit of bronzer on my face, slicked on some ChapStick, and I was ready. No high-maintenance girl here. I hurried down the stairs and snatched the sofa pillows, locking them into my office. Then I topped off my travel mug and eyed Emma's food and water levels.

"I fed and watered her this morning." Greg was still leaning on the counter, watching me.

I leaned down and gave my dog a quick hug, telling her to be good. Locking the back door, I threw the dead bolt for good measure. "I'm ready."

We walked to the front, where Greg paused to lock the door. I glanced over at Esmeralda's house. She either had an overnight guest or someone came early for breakfast. The Range Rover was there again.

Greg took my arm and led me down the stairs. "Not your business."

I gave him a wicked smile as we headed toward the road and up to town. "Maybe not, but it's going to be fun teasing her the next time I see her. I wonder if this Nic guy is moving to the area."

Greg shook his head. "I don't think so. I ran a little background on him the first time I met him and he's big in New Orleans. Like gives-away-a-lot-of-money-to-charities big. He's supposed to be some kind of wealthy socialite, but of course the family runs the fortune-telling business down there. And it's rumored he's involved in a few less-up-front ventures."

I turned to look at him while we were walking. "Like crime stuff?"

Now Greg shrugged. "No one would go that far. He's a very powerful man in the area. But I know he cares for Esmeralda a lot."

"And that's why you checked up on him? To protect her?"

This time he blushed. "I know, none of my business. You can call me on it. I overstepped as her boss. But as her friend, I was concerned."

"You're a good man, Greg King." I took his arm and leaned into him. "I don't see it as overstepping."

"You might not, but Esmeralda would. She'd probably twist my arm for just thinking about checking on her." He exhaled. "I hope she comes back to the station soon. We're dying there without her."

"Well then, I won't tell her what you did." I wrapped my fingers in his. "Your secret's safe with me."

He kissed my hair. "Okay, what do you really want?"

"Who's your primary suspect?" I grinned as we passed by Diamond Lille's. The parking lot tables were empty, but the diner inside was already packed. Locals getting some breakfast before the craziness of the day hit.

He glanced around. We were the only ones on the street.

My heart started pounding. He was actually going to tell me. I couldn't believe this had worked. Most of the time he kept his cop cards very close to his chest. He said it was to protect me, but sometimes I think he just liked the power. "Greg?"

He leaned in close to my ear, paused for a moment, then he whispered, "I have no clue."

I slapped him on the arm. "Greg! I can't believe you."

A woman walking with her goldendoodle chuckled. "You tell him, girl. No sugar until there's a ring on that finger."

I waved as she passed by.

We started walking again. Greg looked behind us at the woman. "Who was that?"

"Not sure, but I think she runs the opal shop down the street by Austin's Bike Shop." I sighed. "She's been at the Business-to-Business meeting a few times. She always has the newest gossip. We'll probably be splitsville by the end of the day."

"We will?"

I shrugged. "She'll tell everyone I'm upset about not being married and how she witnessed a fight between us."

"That wasn't a fight," Greg corrected.

"In Small Town USA that was almost a divorce." I looked both ways and started across the street to the store. Greg followed me. "I'm fine, you don't have to see me to the door."

"Maybe I want to." He took the keys I'd taken from my tote and unlocked the door. Letting me in first, he turned on the lights as I turned off the alarm and headed to the counter to start the coffeepots. He leaned on the counter and put the keys by the register. "Jill?"

"Yes?" I had my back to him as I set up the last pot.

"Do you want me to ask?" His question was soft, but the power of it punched me in the gut. "I mean, I don't want her gossiping to affect us. If you're fine the way things are, then so am I. But if you want, or need something more permanent, I'll ask."

I turned and poured my travel mug coffee into a large, porcelain cup. I walked over and took his hands in mine. "I think we have wedding fever around here. I don't want you to ask me because Aunt Jackie got married. I don't want you to ask me because Amy is getting married. If Justin actually shows back up." Before he could speak, I put a finger on his lips. "And I certainly don't want you to ask to take the wind out of a busybody's sails. We'll know when it's right."

He leaned in and kissed me. Then he leaned back and kept eye contact. "How did I ever get so lucky?"

I laughed. "I'm definitely one of a kind."

The first commuter ambled in. "You're lucky I love your coffee. I had to walk four blocks from the city parking lot just to get my fix."

"Duty calls." I squeezed his hand and went to the counter to make a large café mocha. "I've got a new Nora Roberts that just came in this week. I ordered one just for you."

"You know me too well." The woman nodded at Greg, who tipped his hat at her and left the shop.

No, I was the lucky one. Greg and I were perfect for each other. And that would never change, married or not.

Chapter 20

Over the milling crowd I found my newest employee chatting about a book I knew she'd just finished with one of our regulars. I waved her over to the counter and pointed to the clock. "You need to go if you're going to make the party in time."

Evie glanced at the clock, then nodded. She looked around the still-busy dining room. "Maybe I should stay. I could run over later tonight and take her and Sasha out to dinner."

"Sixth birthdays only come once. Besides, you're the only South Cove representative we're sending to the event. We need you there to deliver our gifts and let Olivia know we still love her." I untied her apron and lifted it over Evie's head. "Go. I'll stay until it calms down. Get on the road before traffic makes you even later. And give both Sasha and Olivia my love."

Evie squeezed me into a big bear hug for a minute. Surprised, I patted her back smelling the vanilla-based perfume she liked to wear.

"Sasha told me that working here would be like having family. I didn't believe her, but it's true." She let me go from the hug and turned to Deek. "And you're sure your mom won't mind you staying in my apartment with Homer this weekend?"

"Are you kidding? She's ecstatic. But hurry back before she changes the locks and I really have to look for somewhere else to live." Deek high-fived his friend. "Have fun with the family."

The shop started slowing down right after Evie left. I sent the temporary help home after giving her a book she'd been checking out since she'd arrived. I was getting ready to leave as well when Meredith walked into the shop. I nodded to Deek. "I'll handle her. You go outside and make sure Aunt Jackie doesn't need anything."

Meredith paused at one of the bookshelves and picked up a recent release. She came over to the register with the mystery and set it on the counter as she dug in her tote for her wallet. "You guys are still busy. I'm dying over there. The foot traffic stopped about four."

"Time for families to get back home and get dinner going." I glanced out the window. "Or if they're without kids, they're at the winery for the night. These festivals seem to close up early for us, especially early in the year like this. Just wait for summer. We'll have crowds on the street until about ten. Then it will die out."

"You really like living here. Owning a business here." She studied me. "Can I get a large coffee to go? Neal took off and the booth isn't being manned right now."

"Sure." I continued talking as I poured her coffee and rang up her purchases. When I told her the cost she handed me a credit card. "I love South Cove. It took some time to grow on me. I kept to myself pretty much the first five years I lived here. Then my friend was murdered and no one was looking into her death. So I did."

"I heard you're something of an amateur sleuth." She lowered her voice. "Have you figured out who killed Nan? Word is your guy listens to you in these things."

I started laughing as I handed back her card and gave her a receipt to sign. "You're kidding, right? Greg hates it when I meddle. That's what he calls it. And I have to admit I get lucky a lot. People somehow like talking to their coffee dealer. I get a lot of whispered secrets."

Her eyes flashed at that, but apparently she must not have been offended as she just tossed her hair and laughed with me. "Baristas are the bartender of the new age."

"I guess so." I glanced around the almost-empty dining room. "Although, the winery's bartender is the one they're confessing to tonight."

She sipped her coffee and slipped off the chair. A clear sign she was done talking.

"Hey, where is Neal? Does he work weekends?"

This time it was her turn to laugh. But the sound was sad, tired somehow. "Not unless you call drinking beer networking. Then yeah, he's working nonstop."

Deek came up to me as she walked out of the shop. "Boss lady, that woman's aura is almost as dark as her husband's."

"Does dark mean sad?" I turned and watched him as he watched her walk away outside the plate-glass window.

He waited until he didn't see her anymore, then turned to me to answer. "No. Dark means anger, violence, and, if you believe in it, evil. Her soul is dark and she's done some bad things, just like her husband."

I thought about the background check Greg had run on Meredith. It had come up clean. So if she had done some evil in this world, it had stayed off the books and out of sight. "Let's close up the outside booth and bring Aunt Jackie inside. She looks lonely out there."

After getting Aunt Jackie situated inside and tearing down the booth outside, I poured a coffee just to stay awake. Even my early-to-bed crash the night before hadn't given me enough energy to get through the day. Deek saw me sipping coffee and came over to sit next to me.

"Why don't you go home? I'll stay until closing. Harrold's on his way over. He just closed up the train station. They had an amazing day, according to Jackie. When he gets here I'll get him to gang up on your aunt and I'll send her home too and close myself. You look like you could sleep for days." He called out to a teenager who had come in with an older woman. He pointed to the middle-grade section. "I had three copies this morning. Hopefully it's still there."

"It better be. I've been waiting for two weeks!" the girl called back.

The woman, who I assumed was her mother, shook her head. "If it wasn't a book she was being so rude about, I'd say something to her. How on earth did you get Candi interested in reading? She's read more this year than since she got out of elementary school."

"You just have to find out what they're interested in. Your daughter loves magic." He smiled at the woman. "What can I help you find?"

"I'm more of an autobiography type. I know what I'm looking for." She smiled at me before she walked toward the stacks. "You have a great staff here."

After they walked away I turned to Deek. "What, do I have 'owner' stitched on my apron?"

"Candi and her mom are locals. All the locals know who you are. I'm surprised you don't know her. She's always buying books when she picks Candi up from the book club." Deek studied my face. "I don't think the coffee is helping."

"I have to agree with that." I stood and finished my cup. "I'm going home. If you need me, call. I can't promise I won't be asleep on the couch."

"I'll only need you in case of one of the four elemental disasters." Deek took the cup from me.

"I'm too tired to guess. What are you talking about?"

He grinned and held up his hand. Pointing to each finger, he said, "Fire, water, wind, or earth. Earthquake, that is."

"You're a typical California kid." I watched as the woman and her daughter stood at the checkout with Aunt Jackie. "Maybe she just isn't an early bird."

"Probably true." He nodded to the door. "Get out of here."

"Yes, sir." I pulled out my phone and texted Greg as I walked. *Walking home. Will be on the lookout for mountain lions and random serial killers. Will text when I arrive. Love you.*

His answer didn't take long and it made me smile as I read it aloud to myself. "'Who are you and why do you have my girlfriend's phone? Love you too, babe.'"

He had been surprised when I started using the "L" word. But now it seemed right. I mean, he said it all the time and had for years. For me, it had taken longer to acknowledge the depth of my feelings. I guess after one failed marriage I was still a little gun-shy on commitment. I felt like my ex-husband and I hadn't spent any time together. Greg and I had a lot of time we committed to our jobs, but it never felt like the casual disregard my marriage had become. Even when he wasn't home I felt his presence in the house. Our home.

Josh and Kyle were taking in the furniture they'd brought out for the display.

Kyle paused as he carried in a lovely antique table. "We had an excellent day today, Miss Gardner; how about you?"

"Sales were great." I nodded to Josh, who turned and ran into the building. I guess he didn't want to talk about the rumor of his possible upcoming nuptials. It was probably for the better anyway. I was too tired to think of creative ways to give him grief. "Go on and get that inside. It looks heavy. I'll talk to you later."

"Have a good night." Kyle turned and followed Josh into the store.

When I was across from the Drunken Artist Studio Meredith was still outside, reading. She looked lonely, and something about it reminded me again about how I'd felt in my first marriage. It wasn't my place to dig into her personal life. At least not yet. But she needed to know if she wanted to talk, I was always available for a quick lunch at Lille's.

I crossed the street and stood in front of her table. She didn't look up. "Hey, Meredith."

She jumped back and almost dropped the book.

"Sorry, I didn't mean to scare you." I tried to hide the smile I felt coming over my face.

She put her hand on her heart. "Well, you did. I guess I was deep into the story already. That's why I'm always an auto-buy for this author. He really knows how to write a story that keeps you turning the pages."

I nodded. I'd read a lot from him in the past. "I've been trying to get him to come to the store for a signing, but I don't think we're a big-enough market to drag him from his Wyoming ranch."

"Well, I'd be there front row if you did." She glanced at the flyers on the table. "Did you need something from me? Don't tell me you want to set up another paint-and-sip class so soon."

"No, but I'm sure we will soon. Maybe I'll schedule the work crew one night as a teambuilding activity." I filed away the thought for another time. "Actually, something you said today reminded me I had a question I wanted to ask you."

"Okay." But from Meredith's face, it didn't look as if she really meant the word.

I decided to give her the sugar first. "I know sometimes it's hard to be in a new place and not, well, have a strong supportive partner. I was married before and now I'm not. So that tells you how my marriage went. Anyway, if you ever want to sit and talk, maybe over lunch at Lille's or just a walk on the beach, I'm a good listener. And I don't gossip."

She smiled, and for the first time I saw the person behind the mask she usually put up. "That's so kind of you. Actually, I need to apologize. I never should have let my frustration at Neal show. Especially to a stranger. We're fine. Really. But I will take you up on that lunch. I'd like to have a few friends around town."

"Then we'll make it a date." I started to walk away, then stopped and turned back. "I'm sorry, but I'm curious. Greg said that when you did your business license for the studio you didn't include Neal on the paperwork. Was he working a different job then?"

And as quickly as it disappeared, the mask reappeared. "That was my bad. I figured that because he was trading at the time, he wouldn't be working with me. The art studio has always been my passion. Neal, he's more of a money guy."

"So he lost his job? That must be hard."

Her lips pressed together. "We manage. We always have."

I realized she wasn't going to say anything else and I'd probably killed my chance of having coffee with her, not to mention a meal. "Well, I'm beat. I don't know about you, but these large events drain me. I'll see you soon."

"Of course we'll schedule that lunch." And then she opened the book and started reading.

As a reader, I knew a dismissal when I saw it. I'd done it to others before too. I started walking toward home and was surprised to see Greg coming out of the police station. He met me at the sidewalk. "What are you doing?" "Walking my best girl home. And I can check on the lower section of Main Street while we walk. The guys have been busy over at the winery for a few hours. This way I kill two birds with one stone." He took my arm.

"Deek called you and told you I was beat, didn't he?" I eyed him suspiciously.

"I've always liked that kid." He chuckled. "But I thought I'd have to catch up with you. I had another call to finish when he phoned in."

"I stopped to talk to Meredith."

He missed a step, but he didn't stumble. "What did you find out?"

"That she doesn't like talking about her marriage. At least when she's not mad at Neal." I waved at Dustin Austin, who was sitting in a lawn chair in front of his shop in a Hawaiian shirt and cargo shorts. He ignored me. Or he was asleep. I couldn't tell with the dark sunglasses he wore most of the time. He owned the bike rental shop and rented the upstairs apartment in his building to Amy. He adored my friend. Me? He tolerated. He'd dated Sadie for a while before his ex-wife came back in the picture. I wondered how he felt about Sadie dating Pastor Bill now. Especially after his wife died. "Sometimes relationships just aren't meant to be."

"Are you still talking about Meredith and Neal?" Greg asked quietly as we passed by the bike shop.

"I don't know. I was just thinking about relationships, and those that work and those that don't." I glanced up at him as we walked. "Did Amy talk to you about Justin?"

"She talked to me the other day. She's worried, but I don't think he classifies as a missing person yet. You saw him in Bakerstown. Did he look suicidal? Or talk like he was getting cold feet and leaving the area?" Greg moved me over on the sidewalk to avoid a group of skateboarders who were using the sidewalk as their own personal path. He called after them, "Watch out for people walking, guys!"

A hand from the last guy flew up and he called back, "Sorry, dude."

"I think I might have talked Marvin into putting at least one side-by-side into next year's budget. The guys are all fighting over being the one assigned to it." Greg pointed to a man walking across the street. "Isn't that Harrold?"

"It is. I heard he was heading up to the shop to get my aunt." I glanced at the street that was still blocked off for cars. "Let's go say hi."

"Sounds good." Greg took my arm and we crossed the road. Diamond Lille's was packed, both inside the diner and the parking lot picnic area they'd set up for the overflow. I saw Carrie bringing out a tray of food and my stomach growled. He looked down at me. "Do we need to stop at Lille's to get some takeout?"

I shook my head. "Nope. I'll eat at home. I've been craving the potato soup that's in the freezer. I'll heat up that. Do you want me to keep a pot on the stove for you?"

"Please. Do we have any dinner rolls? I'm coming home after we close up the festival on Main Street. Toby can deal with the winery revelers tonight. I'm going to be on call, though, so if my phone rings, don't let me sleep through the call." He grinned and waved at Harrold. "Hey, I haven't seen you in days. What have you and the new Mrs. been up to?"

"We had a lovely week in Phoenix, but since we got back, it's been all about the shops. I had a great day today, but I have to say, festivals are tiring. I like it when my shop is quiet and I get one or two customers in a day. Not one or two hundred." Harrold ran a hand through his gray hair. "Jackie and I need to chat about how much we work. I think one of us is going to have to give up their commitments. And before you go crazy, Jill, I think it's going to be me."

"You and my aunt need to make your own decisions." I put my hand on his arm. "Whatever you decide to do will be fine. We'll manage. Actually, Aunt Jackie and I were just talking about hiring someone else to take over her shift. Then all she'll have to do is manage the shop. But if that's too much, we can adjust that too."

"You're a good person." He smiled at me, and not for the first time, I knew my aunt had made the right decision about spending the rest of her days with this man. He was kind and smart and a good person.

"Just make sure you tell my aunt that too." I gave him a hug.

He patted my back. "I'd better get going before she starts to worry. I swear, she times my walk from when I call her to tell her I'm on my way. I think she believes I need to have a companion with me at all times."

"At least she's worrying about you rather than me now." I grinned as he headed toward the shop.

"I like Harrold," Greg said as we started down the hill toward my house. As we got closer, I squinted and pointed to my driveway.

"Who's parked at my house?" If someone had gone through the barricades and parked in my driveway to attend the festival, I was going to have them towed. My house wasn't a public parking spot.

Greg pointed to the man walking toward us. "I think I know who parked there. Look who'd coming up the hill."

Chapter 21

"Hey, guys!" Justin waved at us as he jogged up the hill. Our missing groom had returned.

I waited for him to reach us, then threw my arms around him. "Justin, I am so happy to see you. Are you all right? Where have you been? Have you let Amy know you're home? She's going to be crazy excited to see you."

"I don't understand. You knew I was working on the honeymoon trip. And I called Amy and told her that I'd be gone for a few days." Justin unwrapped my arms around his neck and stared at me and Greg. "Are you telling me you thought something had happened to me? Didn't you tell her I was in Nebraska?"

"I thought you were going to tell her, but I finally did. She just didn't like not talking to you. And your messages were so cryptic. She didn't know what was going on."

I looked at Greg, who jumped in. "Dude, she was about to force me to file a missing person's report on you. The wedding is in a week." He slapped Justin on the back.

"I know. That's why I had to get the honeymoon locked down. It's going to be epic. The waves are crazy right now down at the island." He frowned and glanced up the road toward South Cove. "Are you telling me she's been worried that I disappeared because of the upcoming wedding? She's got to know I love her."

"She didn't know where you were," I said defensively. I didn't like anyone criticizing my friend. "You didn't tell her."

He shook his head. "I couldn't tell her. The honeymoon was supposed to be a surprise. Now I have to ruin the surprise because she thought I was off building some new life without her. Man, this is messed up."

"Go talk to Amy. She'll understand. She'll be ecstatic to see you." Greg slapped him on the back. "Your car can stay in the driveway until you come get it. We'll be opening the road at about seven tonight."

Justin nodded. "Thanks, Greg. Jill." Then he took off at a sprint, this time to find Amy.

We returned to our walk home. "I bet he took off for that island where they sent Amy when Miss Emily died. The cell service out there is crap. And the plane just drops you off and picks you up days later. No wonder he was out of range."

"I hope Amy remembers how worried you were about her during that time." Greg turned us into the driveway and we walked up to the door. He unlocked it and stepped inside first. "I'll let Emma outside and grab a soda, then I'll head back to work."

I followed him into the kitchen and got the soup out of the freezer. Getting it on the stove and starting to thaw took a few minutes. While I did that, I watched Greg take some time with Emma outside. Throwing the ball out to the yard, then watching her run and bring it back. This went on for a while, but then Greg rubbed her head and put the ball down in her baskets of toys, and then she took off to do her check of the yard fence borders. Emma took her job seriously.

Greg came inside and washed his hands at the sink, watching Emma in her wandering. "I miss spending time with her when I'm working so many hours."

"You miss time with my dog. Not me, my dog." I shook my head as I stirred the soup. I put the lid back on the pot, and all of a sudden, Greg had pulled me into a hug and kissed me.

"I make sure I make time for you, no matter how busy I am. I messed up one marriage; I don't want to curse our relationship before it even has a chance to develop." He nodded to the window where Emma still wandered. "She gets the short end of my attention when I'm busy. Which is bad for me, because playing with her calms my blood pressure. So I try to give her a little time when I can."

"She's got you wrapped around her front paw." I patted his chest. "Are you sure you need to go back to work?"

"Sorry, I …" His phone buzzed and he sighed, glancing at the text. "Speak of the devil and it shows up. At least I know you're home. You're staying here, right?"

"Yes. I'm too tired to even try to leave." I nodded to the soup on the stove. "Once I have that in my belly, I'm heading to bed with a book, but I don't think I'll get much read."

He nodded, then let Emma inside. "I'll call you when I'm on my way home."

After Greg left I pulled out my notebook and added notes to the Meredith and Neal page I'd developed. Maybe I should do this on all the local businesses. Who owns what, what they do, who is in their family. That could keep me involved with the people of South Cove. The ones that don't come to the Business-to-Business meetings or shop during my shift. Like Candi's mom. It still burned me that Deek had known her, she'd obviously known me, and I was totally clueless.

The problem with that idea was how I was going to find out about people I didn't know. I wrote down my brilliant, sleep-deprived idea in the notebook. Maybe if I slept on it, the answer would come to me. Some natural woo-woo that was just using more of your brain than you normally did. I'd seen an ARC on the table in the office for a nonfiction book on that subject. Maybe I'd grab it on Tuesday. No, Wednesday. I rubbed Emma behind the ears. "I'm off until Wednesday and we're going running every day I'm not working. Even if Greg has to sit in the parking lot at the beach watching for us during the run."

I closed the notebook and went over to dish up my soup. I brought out the bag of dinner rolls I'd bought at the store and made a quick ham and cheese slider to go with my soup. Then I sat at the table and ate while I read the mystery I'd started the day before.

After dinner I let Emma out one last time, put a load in the washer, and thought about the upcoming week. Amy's wedding was on Saturday, and the rehearsal and dinner were Friday night. Now that Justin was home, I didn't have to worry about him. I could just focus on my chores during the time. I wrote "dry cleaners" on the shopping list because I needed to pick up Greg's suit. Saturday would be all about the wedding, and my aunt was taking my morning work shift. We were running short hours on Sunday, so Deek, Toby, and Evie could handle most of the weekend shifts.

I needed to put an ad in the paper about hiring a new bookish barista. I opened the planner I kept in my tote and added a bunch of stuff to Wednesday. Until then, business owner Jill was on vacation. I needed to be there for Amy. Especially if she actually killed Justin for taking off and scaring her to death. Emma barked at the back door and I closed the planner and put down the pen.

It was time to relax.

* * * *

The next morning the book I'd been reading last night was on my nightstand and both Emma and Greg were missing. But I heard music coming from downstairs, so I got up and got ready for my Sunday at home. I'd have to text Amy to see if we were still on for brunch this morning before I ate with Greg. With Justin home, she might have other plans.

When I got downstairs Toby sat at the table with Greg. They both had coffee and there was a bag of muffins on the table. "Good morning. Bringing treats for an early morning visit? You're learning, Toby."

He laughed. "There are a couple of banana nut and blueberry left. I wasn't sure which one you'd be in the mood for today."

I dug out a banana nut and then went to pour my coffee. Before I sat I eyed the two men. "Is this official chat or can I sit with you?"

"It's official, but you should hear this." Greg pointed to the chair. "Remember the text I got when I left?"

I peeled off the wrapper and broke off a bit of the muffin, setting the rest on a paper napkin I snagged from the bag. "Yep."

"Toby got a call from Meredith. She says her husband is missing."

I frowned as I swallowed the bite I'd just taken. "Yesterday she told me he was at the winery, drinking."

"She says she thought he was as well, but when she went upstairs to her apartment, a suitcase was gone with some of his clothes, five thousand dollars in cash she had stashed in the kitchen in a jar, and a note saying he was done." Greg watched my reaction.

"So why did she call the police over a breakup? You can't drag him back into the marriage." I sipped my coffee, feeling confused.

"Yeah, that's what I told her. She wanted to charge him with stealing the cash, but because they both lived there, it could have been his just as much as it was hers." Greg and Toby shared a look.

I sipped my coffee, thinking about Meredith. Was she just angry and wanted to punish him? Or was there something else? Then it hit me. "She wanted to establish the exact time he left her."

"That's my take too. It's like she needed us to know he was gone." Toby nodded and sipped his coffee. "I know I'm ready for some sleep, but for the life of me, I can't imagine why she did it."

"I asked her yesterday why she hadn't put Neal on the business license application when they moved here. I thought it would be something about their marriage being shaky and she was making a new start. Instead, she said he'd been day trading during that time and she didn't think he'd be part of the business. That it was her dream, not his."

"When did you talk to her yesterday?" Greg narrowed his eyes at me.

"After I left the shop and before I ran into you. Wait, no, that was the second time. She came in and bought a book and coffee. That was when she told me Neal was at the winery, drinking. I went over to invite her to lunch sometime, and she threw me a completely different line about their marriage. I thought it was because she was embarrassed about what she'd said earlier." I finished the muffin and eyed the bag. Instead of grabbing a second one I sipped my coffee. "Maybe she's got a medical condition."

"You mean a mental illness?" Greg clarified.

"Let's just say she changes her story really fast to what she wants to." I crumpled my napkin. "I need to text Amy about brunch."

"It's canceled. She called the house earlier and I talked to her. She says she and Justin need some time to talk." Greg grimaced. "I'd hate to be that guy today."

I dished up a second muffin, blueberry this time. "Okay then, I'm going into the living room to read, unless you need me here. You two can finish your discussion."

"I'm heading to bed." Toby stood and put his cup in the sink. "Thanks for talking with me about this. I didn't want it to wait until Monday if it was important."

Greg stood and followed him to the back door. "It's either important or truly weird. I just haven't decided which one yet. Thanks for stopping in, and thanks for the muffins. Do you want the rest?"

Toby waved his hand, dismissing the muffin bag. "Nope. I'm heading to the gym when I wake up and I don't want to be in a sugar coma when I get there."

My cell rang and I answered it on the way to the couch. "Hey, Amy. Greg told me brunch was off. How are you?"

"As well as could be expected. I mean, yeah, I appreciated him going to the lengths he did for our honeymoon, but I was getting really, really scared. I told him I thought he was dead. Do you know what he did?" Amy didn't wait for my response; she just kept talking. "He laughed. He told me he wasn't going anywhere and I needed to relax. So we're doing a couples money class next week to help with our communication. Do you and Greg want to join?"

I closed the book I'd been setting up to start reading. "I'm sorry. What did you say?"

"There's an intensive, weeklong money class. We'd have to take the Friday one early, but I've already talked to the facilitator and he's willing to move our class to two so we can get it in before the rehearsal dinner. I've heard great things about this class and I think it will help us talk to each other. We get to bring another couple free, so we chose the two of you."

"Thanks for the offer, but honestly, I don't want to go to a personal finance class next week. Besides, with the investigation going on, Greg probably can't get away." I didn't want to upset the bride, but there was no way I was going to fit in a class of any type during the next week. Unless maybe a cooking class. That would be fun. Maybe a wine tasting or pairing with a cooking class. "And I'm really busy getting ready for your wedding, and the shop, and I have to do something for my aunt. She's been calling me for days and I've put her off."

"Sounds like you're full of excuses." Amy laughed. "Okay, I get it. You're afraid to deal with your money issues with Greg. I'm pretty sure he's not going to dump you when he finds out you're terrible with money."

"I am *not* bad with money. I just don't want to take a class." I read the back of the book's blurb while I talked. I just wanted to get back into this world to find out what happened to Cass and her sister. "Look, Greg's waiting for me to go over some things, so I've got to go."

"Now you're lying to me. I just saw him walk past the apartment. You really don't want to talk about taking this class, do you? Please don't tell me you went through all the money Miss Emily gave you."

Darn it, I didn't think she'd be watching the street below her apartment. "Sorry I lied. You're right, I don't want to take this class. But no, it's not because I've spent all Miss Emily's inheritance. I just don't want to take a class this week. I've got Monday and Tuesday off and I thought I'd go into Bakerstown and do a spa day. One where I don't have to study for the final exam."

"Okay, I'll get off your back about this. But don't say I didn't warn you." Amy listed off a ton of work I was supposed to get done before the rehearsal dinner, then said goodbye.

I tossed the notebook where I'd listed out all the new chores for me to do on the coffee table and focused on Emma, who had laid her head in my lap. "I know, girl. Aunt Amy's going crazy and there's nothing we can do about it. Let's curl up and get this book finished. Nobody's going to call me an underachiever then."

My phone rang again, and I considered letting it go to voice mail. But it could have been the shop, or Aunt Jackie, or Greg on the other line. Then I'd feel like crap if something was actually wrong. I picked it up and glanced at the caller ID.

I turned down the stereo I'd just turned on and answered the call. "Hey, Evie, how was the drive?"

"Perfect. But I wanted to tell you that my friend found someone who appeared to be stalking Nan. At least that's what I read in the tweets." Evie had to raise her voice over the screaming children. "I can't stay here long. A laser tag group is just about to go in, and then there won't be any quiet. I'm sending you a link. See what you can do with it."

And with that, either the party place had finally gone silent or I'd lost her call; the other end of the line became dead quiet. My phone beeped and I had a text. I glanced at the website, then opened it up. It was what looked like an advertisement for Nan's Grow Rich Today class. A picture popped up of a slender, young woman sitting at a computer staring into the depths of the screen with a lot of graphs and charts showing. I kept scrolling. Halfway down the comments was what Evie had been talking about. I'd almost missed it as I scrolled.

"Don't waste your time or money. Complete rip-off. The site owner should be tarred, feathered, then shot for putting up something like this. Don't lose your life savings like I did. Scammed to Death." I kept scrolling. Scammed to Death had several posts on this one ad. Mostly in the same vein, but one sent chills down my spine. "I hope they find your cold, dead body soon."

Emma put her paw on my arm and whined.

"Yeah, I agree. That's spooky. Maybe Greg needs to see this." I took a screenshot and sent it off to him. Then I went to check that the lock on the front door was engaged. Emma and I went to the back door and I let her out to do her business. While I waited for her, I put on a sweat shirt that had been hanging on a hook in my kitchen.

The comments from Scammed to Death had chilled me to the bone.

Chapter 22

The next morning a knock on the front door brought me out of my planning mode. With Amy's wedding on Saturday and the new list of to-dos she'd given me as punishment for not taking the finance class with her, I was struggling to find time to get everything done. But I was determined. Planning was like setting up a jigsaw puzzle. You just had to find the right spot for each activity. One that wasn't too long or too short. And if it didn't work, you could always force an activity into a too-small and incorrectly shaped hole.

Greg hated putting puzzles together with me. He said I cheated.

I glanced out the window before opening the door. Esmeralda and a tall, gorgeous hunk of man stood on my porch. A freak storm must have splattered my face with rain because there was no way I was drooling over the dark man. "Esmeralda! Good to see you. Come in and have some coffee with me."

"Okay, but just for a moment. Nic and I are heading out to New Orleans for the week. I need to get away from town gossip and he needs to check on his business investments." She walked into the living room and glanced around. "I don't know if I told you this before or not, but you've done a lovely job turning Emily's house into your home. She would have been so proud."

"Thanks. I just love the house. It feels safe, you know. Safe and comforting." I really hoped she didn't have some sort of angry spook hanging around her right now. I didn't need a ghost issue. I had enough problems right now with the living. "So glad you approve of the changes made. It's a great house. All I did was make it pretty."

"You saved it many times and it's grateful." She held out her hand, fingers wide, and gently touched the wall. "I have to say, you've made an impression on your house. Kind of like what you've done in town. You stand up for what's right. I'm running away from town because I can't deal with the crap, but you just dive headfirst into the problem pool."

"If you say so." I nodded to the kitchen. "Some coffee?" Esmeralda traded a glance with Nic. "I'm sorry, we don't have time. We need to get on the road. But I wanted to tell you something."

"I know where the spare key is and I've been trained in the fine art of feeding your cat." I put my hand on Esmeralda's shoulder and felt a buzz between us. My vision blurred as I tried to get my bearings. When I looked up, Esmerelda's face was blank. She wasn't speaking. "Nic, is she having a seizure?"

He came and took her into his arms, cradling her while she stood in my living room, frozen. Ruining any hope of me thinking bad thoughts about the guy.

"Esmeralda?" I watched as her eyelids fluttered, then recognition came into her gaze. Nic moved her to a chair and held her wrist. He must be checking her pulse. "Esmeralda? Are you okay? Do I need to call an ambulance?"

She took in a breath. "Could I get a drink of water?"

I ran to the kitchen and got her filtered water. I took the glass back into the living room and handed it to her. Emma sat next to her, watching. "Thank you." She took several sips. She stared at me for a long while. Finally, she turned to Nic. "You go get my bags packed in the car. I'll be right there."

After he left I glanced at the kitchen. "I have muffins. Do you want one?"

Esmeralda stood and walked to the door. "Please keep yourself safe. I saw a vision of you and a pair of red shoes. It felt violent."

"I don't have any red shoes. Besides, Greg won't let me walk anywhere alone. And I'm taking Emma with me today to run errands for Amy's wedding." I stood and walked toward her and the door. "Go. Have fun. Don't worry about me."

As she left, I stayed at the door for a long time, watching her leave. Then I closed the door. Esmerelda's visions always bothered me. But usually it was some random comment, like *don't go into the light*. Or some nonsense like that. I'd watched her as she'd gone through this one, and if I didn't believe before, I did now. Now I just needed to figure out what she'd meant by red shoes. Amy had a pair she wore when we went out dancing. But other than her, I didn't think I knew anyone with red shoes. My friends were more sneaker people.

I went back in the kitchen and took out a soda and made my shopping list. I'd leave finding Nan's killer to the professional this time. I had enough to worry about with the shop and Amy's wedding. I didn't need to put myself in some psycho's crosshairs.

And, I thought for the first time, Greg would totally agree.

* * * *

Emma and I returned home just after six. I'd brought water with us and had used the back gate to protect the purchases from her chewing as I'd stopped at each store. We'd even snuck in a quick walk at the park in Bakerstown, with me watching out for anyone who looked the least familiar or dangerous. Emma hadn't even been her usually people-greeting self. She'd stayed right by my side, probably feeding off the unease I'd felt since Esmeralda's visit.

I left the stuff in the car as I went to the front door. All the lights were on in the house and the front door was unlocked. When I turned the knob Emma pushed her way inside and pulled the leash out of my hand. She went running to the kitchen.

She didn't come back out.

I took my cell out, dialed the nine and the first one, then sneaked into the kitchen to see who had absconded with my dog. I glanced in and saw her. A man was bent over, rubbing her ears.

"Hi, Jill. Do you need help bringing in something?" Greg spoke behind me and I twirled, my keys in my hand, and dropped my phone.

Greg picked it up and handed it to me. "It's just me and Toby. Are you all right?"

I collapsed into his arms and the tears fell. I felt like an idiot.

"Jill, you're scaring me. What's wrong?" Greg sounded tense, worried.

I pulled away, rubbed the tears from my face, and shook my head. "Sorry. I've been chased by imaginary ghosts all day. When I saw the house open and figured you were still at work, my imagination took over."

"You're sure you're okay? Esmeralda called and said some weird stuff, and then she told me to watch out for you. That's why I came home. Toby and I are working through some theories, and I figured I could do it here while I cooked dinner. I've got the spaghetti sauce already going." He glanced into the kitchen. "I could send Toby back to the station if that's what's bothering you."

"Are you kidding? Toby's one of mine. No, I've been keyed up since Esmeralda came by. What was the weird stuff she said to you? Hold on one second." I dropped my phone into my tote and walked into the kitchen. "Toby, would you run out and get the stuff from the back of my car? Unless it's food, it can go into the office."

"Sure. I'll go right now." Toby shot up out of his chair and exchanged a look with Greg.

I wasn't sure if it was a nonverbal way of getting his permission or asking if I'd gone off the deep end. I suspected a little of both. When I heard the door close I waved my hand at Greg. "Okay, spill really fast. I don't want Toby to hear this."

"Honestly, all she said was that she'd had some sort of event and I was supposed to watch you closely. I knew you were heading into Bakerstown, so I figured I'd come home and save you the trouble of making dinner. I almost called when I found Emma gone, but something told me she was with you."

I stroked Emma's fur. "Yeah, she was my protector. I don't think I could have gotten through today without her. I took her for a quick walk at that new park down by the courthouse to thank her."

"I'd rather you didn't take strolls until this thing is over, but I get it. Emma needs time too." He rubbed her head. "What is it about red shoes again?"

I froze when he asked the question. "Did Esmeralda bring that up?"

He nodded. "She said it was jumbled. Between Nan's murder and you. But if I saw anyone with red shoes, I was to be wary."

"Not the clearest of predictions." I've heard about people who were just really good at guessing things. I knew that was one of my talents. "Anyway, I watched for red shoes all day. Nothing. Not even a pair of red tennis shoes on the basketball guys."

We heard the door close again and Toby called out, "Everything's in. Do you want me to lock your car?"

"That's fine," I called back. Toby had known that Greg and I needed a private moment. Should I call him psychic for that? "Come back in the kitchen."

"You sure have a lot of flowers and beads and that fluffy fabric." He sat at the table and rubbed his hands like the cooties from the wedding decorations were going to stick on him and he'd be swept up into the whole marriage thing.

I pulled out my to-do list and started marking things off. "It's not contagious, but thanks for grabbing all that. Amy sent me to almost every store in Bakerstown for that stuff. The reception hall is going to be a bear to clean up when this is done."

"Glitter?" Greg asked from his place at the stove.

I laughed as I marked the last thing off my list. I wouldn't have to go back to town tomorrow, which meant I could spend the day reading. Or cleaning house. "Like Joseph's coat of many colors."

They both looked at me blankly. I shook my head. Apparently I'd been the only one to pay attention in Sunday school.

"Anyway, Toby was just walking through the timeline of the night Nan was murdered. I'll have him start again at the beginning and you can tell me if something is off." Greg got out a loaf of French bread and started cutting it for garlic bread. "Go ahead, Toby."

"Well, the victim and her husband were at a paint-and-sip party at the Drunken Artist Studio. The victim appeared to be inebriated, according to several witnesses."

I nodded. "She was three sheets to the wind. And Steve wasn't very happy with her."

Greg nodded. "I got that feeling too. I guess he was ready for her to move on from the grief. Nan wasn't."

"I can't believe she was still teaching her classes if she was that upset." I stood and got a soda out of the fridge.

"According to Steve, she wasn't. Most of her classes were online and self-taught. She just maintained the materials. He said she'd been doing the minimum for months," Greg said.

"Well, from the reviews she had on line, it showed. She was getting hammered by people who didn't think her classes were any good. There was one who said he lost his life savings." I shook my head. "Day trading seems as bad as gambling. I can't believe it's legal."

"She seemed to be making good money with the classes." Toby pointed to his screen. "According to the tax records, her company grossed over six figures last year. That's a lot of classes."

"That's a lot of stupid. People go to school for years to understand finance. One online workshop isn't going to give you the tools to win against the big investment companies." Greg shook his head. "I feel sorry for her students. Maybe I can talk to Steve about taking the site down."

"The Facebook page is already gone. Some of the comments are pretty upset with her and her class. Taking down the website will at least stop more people from thinking it's a get-rich-quick pill." I sipped my soda. Something was nagging at me.

"The name of the company is Grow Rich Today. I'm surprised someone didn't sue her for false advertising." Toby snorted. "The only one who seemed to be growing rich was Nan."

My head was clanging for attention, like the bells from old *Tom and Jerry* cartoons. Something I was missing. And it was right here. Clang, clang, clang.

"So you agree that there's a lot of circumstantial evidence pointing to Neal Cole?" Greg was asking Toby, but he was looking at me.

"Neal?" The thought of being near that man made my skin crawl. He'd tried to rob me. Okay, so he'd thought about robbing me and would have done it if the till had been unlocked.

"You said it yourself; he's a failed day trader. The idea to start trading must have been from one of the ads for the class. Then, when she showed up all drunk at the party, he waited until we were all gone and killed her. Perfect crime." Toby slapped his hands together. "Case solved."

"Except he didn't kill her at the studio. He drove her and Steve home, remember? We were talking to him when he said he was going to take their keys and he'd make sure they were home safe." I couldn't believe I was arguing his case. "It doesn't seem like he would be worried about them driving a couple of blocks drunk if he was planning to kill her anyway. He seemed upset about the loss of their son."

"Jill's right. Nan came back to the studio. Why?" Greg tapped his pen on the table. "Did anyone else talk to Nan during the class?"

I tried to remember the night. Nan had been so drunk, everyone had been ignoring her. Except Neal and Meredith. I realized what had been bothering me. "Meredith talked to both Steve and Nan after Neal left the room for a while. And she was really upset at Neal for drinking. Maybe that was just the cover. Maybe she was upset about him losing the money. She decided to move here on her own, filling out the business license in her name. Maybe this was her escape from the marriage, but she decided to give him one more shot."

Greg was staring at me.

"Or maybe not. I guess if you're married to someone, you can be mad at them and love them all at the same time." I tried to backtrack and looked at Toby. He was watching me too. "Okay, you all are freaking me out. Stop staring at me."

Greg turned to Toby. "If we take the same motivation and put it on Meredith, does the answer still come out the same?"

"Actually, it fits better. Neal went to the winery after he dropped off the Gunters. We had issues with his timing. He walked home and Darla verified his car was there the next morning. We thought he just got a ride back to the apartment. But what if he was walking back? He would have gone to the apartment up the back stairs." Toby stared at Greg. "Why didn't we see this before?"

"Because Meredith steered us to Neal. He seemed like the perfect killer." Greg kissed me on the top of my head. "Sorry, honey, I've got to go back to work and bring in Meredith. We have a few more questions for our local art teacher."

I glanced at the half-cooked meal. "What about dinner?"

Greg looked at Toby.

Toby sighed and stood. "I'll go pick her up if you bring me dinner when you come to meet me. We can hold her for a few hours before she's due a phone call. And don't forget to bring garlic bread."

"I'll pack it myself." I stood and put a pot of water on to boil. We didn't have long to have dinner, but we had at least an hour.

"I'll call you when I'm back at the station." Toby picked up his tablet and rubbed Emma's head. "See you, Jill. And thanks for dinner."

"You're welcome, but Greg did most of the work." I watched as he left by the back door to climb into the police cruiser he'd brought to the house. "Do you really think it might be Meredith?"

"I'm convinced of it. It had to be someone who knew that Nan was even here. She could have been killed in her own house for months. But she died in South Cove. Where only a few people knew her." He rubbed his face. "That's no coincidence."

* * * *

I got the call right before I went to bed. I'd cleaned the kitchen, texted Amy about what I'd gotten in town. I knew she couldn't respond because she was at her money class. I'd just finished rewatching a movie about wizards and muggles, one of my favorites, when the phone rang.

"She confessed. Mostly because I got her mad, but a confession it was. Now she's clammed up and asked for an attorney, so as soon as I get thing squared away, I'll be home."

"Her anger gives her away. That's when she told me about Neal. When she wasn't in control of what and how she said things." She'd known Greg was head of the police here. She'd been playing us since she'd moved here. That was the reason for the free painting class. Now I didn't even want to hang my painting.

"You're right. That's exactly why she confessed." He chuckled. "I played her like a fiddle. You'll never guess what she was wearing when Toby picked her up."

"Red stilettos?"

"Seriously, Esmeralda does have a gift." He chuckled. "See you soon."

I turned off most of the lights, leaving one on in the library for Greg. Amy's wedding was this weekend. It was time to crash so I could help my friend tomorrow.

Chapter 23

Sitting at the reception at a table covered with glitter and flower petals, I watched Justin twirl Amy around the dance floor. Her smile told the whole story. She was ecstatically happy. The day had been beautiful. All the stress had been worth it. We'd had breakfast together, but neither one of us ate much. I brought my dress with me to the venue, and we got ready together. Amy's stylist had come and brought a makeup person. I didn't even know Amy *had* a stylist. Greg came back from the lobby and sat behind me. I leaned into him and he wrapped his arms around me. "It was a beautiful wedding."

"Yes, yes, it was." He kissed my neck. "And you look beautiful too. If I haven't told you that yet today."

"A girl can stand to hear it more than once." I turned toward him. "Was that Esmeralda?"

He laughed. "Maybe you do have the sight. Yes, it was our neighbor, and she's on her way home. She's coming back to work on Monday. And I'm so happy, I gave her a raise."

I nodded over toward Marvin and Tina, who were at a small table by themselves. Amy had taken the easy way out. They probably liked their own company best anyway. "You could ruin his night if you wanted."

He squeezed my waist. "Sometimes you're a troublemaker, you know that, right?"

"Sometimes." I was watching Aunt Jackie and Harrold dance now as well. "Keep an eye out for a new barista for me. Preferably not someone who works with you."

"I concur. Moving things around for us to leave is always hard with Toby. I was surprised he brought Evie to the wedding. I didn't realize they were dating." He waved at our shared employee as he walked over to the buffet table. Again.

"They aren't. That's why they came together. That way, no one had unrealistic expectations and they could both have fun." I watched as he piled his plate full of appetizers. "I think she's too close to Sasha for him to think of her as anything other than a friend."

"He's still not over her, is he?"

I smiled as Toby walked by, a miniburrito in his mouth. He grinned but didn't stop to talk. The music was too loud to really chat anyway. Greg and I were really, really close and we were having problems hearing each other. "Not even close. He says he is, but you can see it in his eyes sometimes. Love can really suck at times."

"And it can be wonderful." He pointed to Justin and Amy. "They're going to be amazing together."

"I hope so. She's been in love with him since she met him." I glanced at my watch.

"You ready to leave?"

"Soon. I hate leaving Emma this long. I've been gone all day." I nodded to the wedding couple. "But I have to make sure all the traditions are done. And I think she still has to throw the bouquet."

"Are you going to catch it this time?" He spun me around so he could see my face.

"It's up to fate, not me. Besides, I have to have someone else who's invested in the outcome."

He stared at me. "You don't think I'm invested?"

"I was talking about catching the bouquet. We're a long way from a wedding." My stomach was clenching. I didn't want him to propose because he thought he had to.

He patted his chest pocket. "I guess I'll just keep this for another time then."

"You don't have a ring in there," I challenged him, and reached out and felt a hard box inside the suit Greg wore.

"You shouldn't challenge me when I'm serious." He held my gaze. "Is this a good place or a bad place? I don't want to steal Amy and Justin's thunder."

"It's pretty loud. Maybe we should go out to the garden. There's a bench by the rose trellis." My voice quavered a bit. Was this really happening?

He stood and held out his hand. "Let's go to the garden, then."

Chocolate Gooey Butter Cake

Dear readers,
I have to say, when I moved to St. Louis I didn't get the gooey butter cake craze. It just seemed too buttery, too wet, too gooey. Maybe it was for kids. Maybe that was the magic. Because the ones I tried were way too sweet. Then I made a chocolate gooey butter cake for Thanksgiving. And I totally fell in love. So here's my gooey butter cake. Sorry it's not the original, but everything is better with a little chocolate, right?

Ingredients:
2 sticks butter, melted (keep separate)
1 package chocolate cake mix
3 eggs (one egg for bottom cake layer two eggs for filling layer)
1 package (8-ounce) cream cheese, softened
1/4 cup cocoa powder
16 ounces powdered sugar
1 teaspoon vanilla extract

Heat oven to 350 degrees and grease a 9-inch-by-3-inch round cake pan.
Mix together the cake mix, 1 egg, and 1 stick melted butter until well blended.
Pat the mixture into prepared pan and set aside.
In a stand mixer on medium speed, beat the cream cheese until smooth. Add the remaining 2 eggs and the cocoa powder until well mixed.
Lower the speed of the mixer and add the powdered sugar, then mix. Slowly add the remaining stick of melted butter, then mix. Add vanilla and continue to beat the mixture until smooth.
Pour filling over cake mixture in pan. Bake for 40 to 50 minutes.
Cake center should still be a little gooey when finished. Remove cake from pan and let it partially cool on a wire rack before cutting into pieces.
Enjoy with whipped cream.

Plenty more to come in South Cove
in the next Tourist Trap Mystery
coming soon!
And don't miss more mysteries from
Lynn Cahoon
The Kitchen Witch series
The Farm-to-Fork series
and
The Cat Latimer series
available now!

Printed in the United States
by Baker & Taylor Publisher Services